"Now s[...] [...] all men were [...] be-cause thralls at least have [...] and protection in law. Suppose all men were slaves except for one master and his soldiers. And suppose that master had the worst kind of madness, finding his greatest pleasure in the misery and degradation, the torture, of his slaves. An emperor who conquered only to enjoy the cries, the whimpers, the begging for mercy of those he ruled. A man who had lived very long and has a great army." Raadgiver leaned toward Nils. "What would you do if you lived in a land like that?"

"I have never thought of such a thing," Nils answered. "Where is that land?"

"Right now it is far to the southeast," Raadgiver answered. "But someday, perhaps soon, it may include all of Europe, even Denmark.

"And what we want you to do is kill that man."

Look for these other TOR BOOKS by John Dalmas

HOMECOMING
TOUCH THE STARS: EMERGENCE (with Carl Martin)
THE VARKAUS CONSPIRACY
THE SCROLL OF MAN (coming in January 1985)

The Yngling

By John Dalmas

TOR

A TOM DOHERTY ASSOCIATES BOOK

THE YNGLING

Copyright © 1971 by Pyramid Publications, Inc.

Reprinted by arrangement with the Author

A TOR Book

Published by Tom Doherty Associates,
8-10 West 36 Street,
New York, N.Y. 10018

Cover art by James Gurney

First TOR printing: October 1984

ISBN: 0-812-53473-5
CAN. ED.: 0-812-53474-3

Printed in the United States of America

THE YNGLING

1.

Nils Hammarson stood relaxed among a few freeholders, thralls, and two other sword apprentices, watching two warriors argue in the muddy beast trail. In his eighteenth summer, Nils's beard was still blond down, but he stood taller and more muscular than any sword apprentice of the Wolf Clan for many years. And sword apprentices were selected at puberty from among all the clan, even the sons of thralls, for their strength and keenness.

The argument they listened to was personal and not a clan dispute. The clans of the Svear had met to hold a ting, and trade, and take wives. And though the ting now had closed, clan feuds were in abeyance until the clans dispersed to their own lands. Only personal fights were allowed.

The warrior of the Wolf Clan was smaller and his beard more gray than brown, but he refused to back down before his larger, younger adversary. The warrior of the Eagle Clan suddenly shot out his large left hand to the necklace of wolves' teeth, jerked forward and down. The older man saw the move coming and kept his balance, al-

though the leather thong bit hard into his neck
sinews. He swung a knobby fist with his heavy
shoulder behind it, driving a grunt from the
younger. For a moment they grappled, each with a
knife in his right hand and the other's knife wrist in
his left. Briefly their arms sawed the air, their
bare feet carrying them in a desperate dance, muscles bunched in their browned torsos while callused
heels strove to trip.

Then strength told, and the warrior of the Wolf
Clan toppled backward. His breath grunted out as
his heavier opponent fell on him; his left hand lost
its sweaty grip and quickly the other's blade drove
under his ribs, twisted upward through heart and
lungs. For a brief moment, as his blood poured
over his opponent's hand and forearm, his teeth
still clenched and his right arm strained to stab.
Then his body slackened, and the warrior of the
Eagles arose, panting and grinning.

Most of the watchers left. But Ragnar Tannson
and Algott Olofson still stood, glaring at the killer
of their clansman, for they were sword apprentices
and nearly matured. There were narrow bounds
on what they could say to a warrior, however, for
warriors were forbidden to kill outside their class
unless the terms of the feud specifically allowed.
And this was not a feud at all yet, although it
would probably be proposed and accepted as one.

But the wish to kill was on their faces.

The Eagle warrior looked at them, his grin
widening to show a dead tooth that had turned
gray. "I see the cubs are beginning to feel like
real wolves," he said. His eyes moved to Nils
Hammarson who stood, still relaxed, a slight
smile on his face. "All but the big one, eh? A

thrall's son I'll bet, strong as an ox and almost as quick. Or maybe your blood runs hot, too, but you hide it."

Nils shifted his weight easily, and his voice was casual. "Nay, Du." For a sword apprentice to address a warrior with the familiar pronoun bordered on insolence. "I was memorizing your face. The old man lying there is my kinsman, Olof Snabbhann, and in one year I'll be wearing warrior's braids." He paused. "Not that everyone with braids deserves to be called warrior."

The Eagle warrior's eyes narrowed in his darkening face and he strode toward the youth. He aimed a fist at the blond head. But the fist that met him was quicker; his steel-capped head snapped back and he fell heavily in the trampled mud, his head at an odd angle. Algott Olofson knelt by him quickly, then rose. "You've killed him," he said gravely.

But the ting was over and crimes between clans would not be judged again until the next year. Therefore, Nils was free to go home. He spent his summer as any sword apprentice would, hunting bear and wild bulls, rowing out into the long lake to draw in nets, and particularly training, with his ring mates. They lifted boulders and wrestled. They swung, parried, and thrust at shadow enemies with heavy iron practice swords twice the weight of a war sword. They sparred with birch swords and weighted wooden shields, and sent arrows at staves marked with the totems of other clans.

But if his activities were normal, the subtler things of life weren't. Everyone knew that at the next ting he would be judged, and when one remembered this, it was sometimes hard to be at ease with him. He could be executed. Or he could be labeled a renegade, to live alone in the forest without clan protection. In that case Eagle warriors would surely hunt him down and kill him. The least sentence possible was banishment.

Nonetheless, Nils Hammarson seemed about as always—relaxed, mild-spoken and observant. He had changed mainly in one respect. Before, in sparring, he had usually been content to parry and counter, seldom pressing a vigorous attack. Although he invariably won anyway, the drillmaster had sometimes thrashed him for this. Now, without ferocity but overpoweringly, his birch club-sword thrust and struck like the weapon of a Bärsärk, making his bruised and abraded ringmates exceed themselves in sheer self-defense. Their drillmaster, old Matts Sväädkunni, grinned widely and often, happier than anyone could remember. "*That* is how a Wolf should fight," he would bellow. And he had a new practice sword forged for his protégé, heavier than any other in the clan.

Late in September, when the cold weather came, the sword apprentices butchered cattle, drinking the steaming blood, smearing each other with gore and brains, and draping entrails about their necks and shoulders so they would not be squeamish in battle. And in late October, after the first heavy snow, they slipped the upturned toes of their ski boots under the straps and hunted moose and wild cattle in the forests and muskegs. After that, as was customary for sword apprentices, Nils Hammarson wrapped cheese and meat in his sleeping bag of glutton skins, took his bow and short sword and went for days at a time into the rugged, uninhabited hills above Lake Siljan. But now he did not hunt the wolf, their clan totem, with a ringmate. In fact he did not hunt so much as travel, northwest even into the mountains of what tradition called Jämtland, where long glaciers filled the valleys. The great wanderer of the Svear, Sten Vannaren, told that the ice had moved down the valley more than three kilometers in five years. Someday, he said, the ice will reach the sea.

Nils would have liked to have seen the glaciers in summer when the land was green, but he expected never to be here again.

Not that he would be executed—struck down like an ox to have his head raised on a pole at the ting. The circumstances had not been that damning. And this belief was not born of hope, nor did it give rise to hope. It was a simple dispassionate evaluation that would prove correct or incorrect, but probably correct.

And if it came down to it, he would escape. To his knowledge, no one had ever tried to escape a sentence of the ting. It would be considered shameful and jeopardize future lifetimes. But Nils did not believe it would be shameful for him, nor did his blood quicken at the thought.

He simply knew that he was not intended to have his head lopped off before the clan.

In July, after the hay was cut and stored, another ting was held. It heard a number of complaints and disputes. Warnings were given. Feuds were approved. Fines of cattle, potatoes and grain were levied, and backs flogged. A hand was cut off. And from a copper-haired head, runnels of blood dried on a pole at the ting ground.

At the trial of Nils Hammarson, two witnesses were heard: Ragnar Tannson and Algott Olofson. They were Nils's friends and ringmates, but no one would lie to a ting. After their testimony, the council sat in quiet discussion in its tent for a time, then emerged and mounted the platform of hewn timbers. Warriors and freeholders covered the broad and trampled field. Axel Stornäve, chief of the Svear, arose from his carved throne and stood before the clans in his cloak of white owl skins. His voice boomed, showing little sign of his sixty years.

"Nils Hammarson angered a warrior," he said. "But his speech was within bounds, though barely.

"Nils Hammarson struck a warrior whose attack on him was without arms and not deadly.

"Nils Hammarson killed a warrior, though without intention.

"Nils Hammarson is stripped of all rights but one, beginning with the second new moon from now. By that time he must be gone from the lands of the tribes. If he is not gone by the second new moon, he will be declared a renegade. Notice of this judgment will be sent to the Jötar and the Norskar, and they will not take him in.

"One right is retained. Nils Hammarson is in his nineteenth summer and has fulfilled his sword apprenticeship. Where he goes he will be an outlander, unprotected by clans or laws. Therefore, when the ting is over, his hair will be braided and he will leave the land as a warrior."

The Eagle Clan grumbled at this leniency, but the ting had ruled. Three days later, Ulf Vargson, chief of the Wolf Clan, plaited the hair of the six Wolf sword apprentices who were in their nineteenth summers and gave them their warrior names. And Nils Hammarson became Nils Järnhann, "Iron Hand."

2.

Neovikings. The neovikings were members of a primitive, post-plague Terran culture that evolved in Sweden and Norway after the Great Death that left less than 10^{-4} of the pre-plague population alive. They consisted of three tribes: the Norskar in southern Norway, the Jötar in southern Sweden, and the Svear in central Sweden. . . .

The term "neovikings" was applied to them by the post-plague psionic culture known as the "kinfolk." In some respects neoviking was not an apt term, for they were not sea rovers. They were primarily herdsmen, although hunting and fishing rivalled livestock in their economy and they practiced some agriculture. Perhaps their outstanding cultural feature was their unusually martial orientation, and in this they did somewhat resemble the medieval vikings. Tribe warred against tribe, and clans carried on bloody feuds.

They increased despite their love of bloodshed, however. Taboos, tribal laws and intertribal agreements restricted the causes of fighting, its circumstances and practices. . . .

History. . . . The rapid climatic deterioration finally became critical. They found it necessary to store increasing quantities of forage as the season of pasturage became shorter. Crops became poorer, and some lands that had been farmed became too waterlogged and cold to grow crops. Had this happened three or four centuries earlier, they might have lapsed into a purely hunting and fishing culture, but they had become too numerous and sophisticated for that. A coastal clan, familiar with fishing boats, began to build vessels large enough to carry effective raiding parties to other parts of Europe. A rather close analog of the medieval viking culture might have developed, had not. . . .

(From the *New School Encyclopedia*, copyrighted A.C. 920, Deep Harbor, New Home.)

3.

It was no fishing boat, but a broad cargo ship made for the open sea and a full thirty meters long. The prow turned upward, and the end was carved and painted in the likeness of a sea eagle with wings partly folded. The water was choppy, and a brisk southwest wind blew. The ship's course being southwesterly, the sail was furled and the crew leaned into the oars, their brawny backs wet with sweat. Through the blue sky moved flocks of small white clouds. The sun sparkled off millions of facets of sea surface, making Nils's eyes squint against the glitter. A low shore, featureless at first in the distance, drew gradually nearer, becoming low dunes backed by rolling heath. Woods of stubby oaks took form in some of the hollows. Nils Järnhann had never seen the sea before, nor oak woods, and stood absorbing the beauty and novelty.

A break appeared in the dunes and became the mouth of a stream that flowed out of the heath. A short distance up the stream, on its south side, a town became visible past the shoulder of a dune. A lookout called down from the mast, and the stroke strengthened as the oarsmen began a chant, for this was their homeplace.

When the ship was tied to the wharf of oak timbers, the oarsmen became stevedores, and under the captain's direction began to unload the pine planks that made up their cargo. A movement caught the captain's eye and he turned to see his passenger approaching. The captain was a big man, but this fellow was bigger—more than a hundred and ninety centimeters tall, he judged, with muscles impressively thick and sinewy even to one accustomed to the sight of brawny oarsmen. His corded torso was bare and brown beneath the simple leather harness that supported his sword belt. Soft deerskin breeches were wrapped close around his calves by leather strips, and his callused feet were bare. A necklace of wolves' teeth hung on a thong across his thick chest and the skin of a wolf's head was laced onto his steel cap. Straw-colored braids hung to his shoulders. Obviously a warrior of the northmen, and a new one, the captain thought, noting the sparse soft beard and mustache so out of character with the physique.

Nils addressed the captain. "Will you hire me to help unload cargo?"

"When did warriors start hiring out as labor?" the captain asked.

"When they have spent their last coin for passage and need something to eat."

"All right. One krona when the cargo is all on the wharf, if you work well and make no quarrels. Otherwise, nothing, and the arrows of the town wardens if there is trouble." The captain believed in giving a man a chance and also in making things clear from the beginning. And fear wasn't a trait of his.

He matched Nils with a thick-armed man of medium height, and without words they made a point of pride in carrying bigger loads than any other pair working. Even with the breeze, all of them were soon dripping sweat—a familiar and agreeable enough experience both to oarsmen and warrior. Soon Nils removed helmet, harness, and sword, laying them with his other things on a rowing bench forward.

Well into the afternoon one of the crew suddenly shouted, "Hey! Stop!" A youth, who had boarded unnoticed, leaped from the gunwale carrying Nils's scabbarded sword. The captain, on the wharf supervising the piling, bellowed, drew his knife and threw it, but it clattered uselessly on the cobblestones. Nils's bare feet hit the wharf running. The thief was quick; he reached a corner and sprinted out of sight. A moment later Nils made the turn, and the thief realized he had dangerously underestimated both the weight of the sword and the speed of a barbarian who had spent much time running on skis. He drew the sword as he ran, then turned and faced his pursuer. Nils stopped a few meters from him, and seconds later several of the crew ran up, panting, to stand near.

"I can stand here as long as you can," Nils pointed out matter-of-factly. "If you try to run away again with the sword, I will easily catch you. And if you run at me to kill me, you won't be able to. But if you lay the sword down and walk away, I'll let you go."

The thief scowled and licked his lips nervously. He was Nils's age, lean and wiry. Suddenly he rushed at Nils, the sword raised to one side in both hands, ready to swing. The sailors scattered, and in that instant Nils sprang high above the swinging blade. A hard foot shot out, a powerful thigh driving the heel into the thief's chest and hurling him backward. He skidded on his back and lay still.

"What must I do now?" Nils asked.

"Is he dead?" asked the sailor that Nils had worked with.

"He's dead all right," Nils assured him, without needing to examine the body.

"Well then, there's nothing to do. A warden's likely to come around and question us, and we'll tell him what happened. He'll have the body taken away and that'll be the end of it. There won't be any trouble for you, if that's what you're wondering about."

Nils and the sailor began walking back to the wharf.

"And what about his clan?" Nils wondered.

"What's a clan?"

"A clan is, well ..." Nils had never thought about this before. It was as natural a part of life as eating or breathing. "A clan is like the family, in a way, but much bigger, and the members fight for each other and take vengeance if need be."

"In Denmark we don't have clans. Countrymen have lords. But townsmen and sailors are loyal mainly to their bellies."

"And I won't be judged at a ting?"

"Ting? I've never heard the word." The sailor paused. "Swordsman, let me give you some advice. The world you've come to is a lot different from your barbarian backcountry. Its ways and even its speech are different. You and I can talk together partly because Danish and Swedish aren't so different in the first place, but also partly because we sailors are used to going to ports in Jötmark and adapting our speech for Swedish ears. But most Danes have never heard a Swede, and you won't find it so easy to talk to them at first. And if you travel farther, to the German lands for example, you won't understand their ways or anything they say. If you're going to travel in civilized lands, you'd better learn something about their customs; otherwise, even a man like you will find only hardship and death.

The inn loomed two-stories high in the darkness and was made of planks instead of logs. The shutters were open, lighting the street in front of the windows and leaving nothing between the noise inside and the passersby outside. Nils had a krona in his pouch, strong hunger in his gut, and the sailor's words in the back of his mind as he moved lightly up the steps.

The noise didn't stop as he crossed the room, but the volume dropped a few decibels and faces turned to look. The innkeeper stared a moment at the bizarre but dangerous-looking barbarian wearing a pack with a shield on it, a slung bow, and a sword. Then he walked over to him.

"Do you want a bed, stranger?"

The sailor had been right. Nils understood the question, but Danish speech was different. He might indeed have trouble understanding longer speech or making himself clear. At any rate, he would speak slowly.

"No, only food," he said. "The ground will have

to be my bed, or else I'll run out of money too soon."

The innkeeper eyed him narrowly and leaned a stout forearm on the bar top. "You plan to sleep in the open, if I take your meaning." He too spoke slowly now. "In that case, more than your money may disappear; your life's blood also. If you don't know that, then the world is a dangerous place for you."

"I have been robbed already today," Nils said. "Are there so many thieves in Denmark?"

"There are thieves everywhere, and towns have far more than their share. Are you the barbarian who crushed the chest of Hans fra Sandvig with his bare foot?"

"If that was his name."

"Well, that's a service worth a free meal and a mug of beer with it," the innkeeper said, and called a waiter. "Dreng, take this man to a table. Give him a mutton pie and a mug of beer, and when the mug is empty, fill it a second time."

Nils leaned over the pie with busy fork. He was aware that someone stood near the table watching him, and his eyes glanced upward occasionally as he ate. The watcher, of middle height, wore his yellow hair cropped close, and unlike the townsmen, carried a short sword at his hip.

After a bit the man spoke. "You are a Swede," he said, "the one who killed an armed thief with only your foot." He spoke a hybrid Swedish-Danish, from lips not at home with either, accented with a crisp treatment of the consonants.

Nils straightened from his plate. "Yes, I'm from Svealann. And you are no Dane either."

"No, I'm a Finn—in our language we say Suomalainen."

"I've heard of the Finn land," Nils said. "Svea fishermen are sometimes driven there by storms. What do you want of me?"

"I am traveling alone in the world, and it's healthier not to travel alone. You're traveling too."

"I'm used to traveling alone," Nils countered, "even in land without people, where wolves and bears hunt. I've slept buried in the snow without harm."

"Yes, but you're not in your homeland now. In Denmark there aren't any wolves or bears, but to the outlander, men are more dangerous."

"Where are you going?" asked Nils.

The Finn did not answer at once. "I don't know," he said at last. "I seek a thing of great value and go where my search takes me."

"Where your search takes you," Nils echoed musingly. "Suppose that's not where I want to go?"

"I believe it's as good as any for you," the Finn replied. "Because if I'm right, you don't have any place in mind. Also, you don't know the ways and tongues of the world, and need a guide and teacher."

Nils leaned back, a grin on his boy's face. "You're the third today who's pointed out my ignorance to me. I believe you must be right. But tell me, why do you think I have no place in mind?"

"Well, for one thing, I suspect you don't know of any places. But regardless, you're a warrior, and among your people it is good to be a warrior. Few warriors would leave the fellowship of their clan to wander alone in the world. Probably you were exiled, most likely for killing outside the bans."

"Sit down," Nils said, motioning to a chair across

from him. "Now I'll ask another question." His
speech was easy and assured, like that of a chief
twice his age. "You say you seek a thing of great
value. If it's so valuable, others may seek it with
armed men. And if someone already has it, it may
be strongly guarded. What will we do if we find
it?"

"I don't know," the Finn answered. "I can only
wait and see." He paused, started as if to speak,
paused again, then said it. "You're a barbarian,
young and very ignorant, but you are not simple.
Not simple at all. Which is so much the better, for
you'll be much more than a man to frighten
robbers."

Nils ate, without saying any more, until the mug
was empty and the plate wiped clean. He signaled
the waiter with the empty mug. "I'll travel with
you awhile," he said to the Finn. "For you were
right about me in every respect; I am an outcast,
and have nothing better to do. But there's a lot I'll
want to know, about you and your quest as well as
about the world, and I won't promise that our
paths will continue together." He half rose and
held out his large, thick right hand. "I am Nils
Järnhann."

"Iron Hand. I believe it." The Finn retrieved his
own. "And I am Kuusta Suomalainen."

4.

Nils and Kuusta walked all day, and never had Nils seen such farmland. The fields covered more land than the forests—broad fields of oats and barley, nearly ripe. Tame trees in rows, which Kuusta said bore fruit called apples. Large herds of cattle. Even the forests were unfamiliar to Nils. Most of the trees had broad leaves and were larger than the birches of home. And although some of the pines seemed familiar, most of the needle-leaved trees were strange, too, and large.

And there were sheep, which Nils had never heard of before. Kuusta said that sheep were foolish and easily caught and killed by wild dogs, which the Danes hunted relentlessly so that they were cunning and cowardly. In Sweden and Finland, he pointed out, it would be impossible to keep sheep because of the wolves and bears. But the fur of sheep, called wool, could be made into warm clothing, and it was this most Danes wore instead of hides.

Then Kuusta talked about the languages of men. They were as many as the kinds of trees that grow in Denmark, he said, and no one could learn any large part of them. But there was one that could be spoken by most people in most lands, at least to some extent, and was used by traders and travelers outside of their own countries. It was called Anglic, and was easy to learn. He taught Nils a few Anglic phrases, starting with: "I am hungry. Please give me food. Thank you."

During the day they saw two small castles. Kuusta insisted they avoid these, leaving the road and keeping to the woods or hedgerows to pass them.

In the early evening they made camp and Kuusta went out to set rabbit snares. While he was gone, Nils saw a deer, sent an arrow through it, and drank the warm nourishing blood. When Kuusta returned and saw the deer, he became ill at ease, saying the Danish lords forbade their killing by anyone but themselves. When they caught a peasant who had killed a deer, they ordinarily knotted a rope around his neck and pulled him off the ground to kick and jerk and swell in the face until he died. Then they'd leave him there, his toes a few centimeters from the ground, and the magpies or crows would relieve him of his eyes, and in the night wild dogs might come and feast on his guts.

Nonetheless, the deer was dead, and neither man was inclined to let it go to waste. They built a small fire, roasted the heart and liver and tongue, and ate while more meat roasted for the road. Then they put out the fire and rolled up in their sleeping robes.

"Now it's time for questions and answers," Nils said in the darkness, "about the thing you're hunting for."

Kuusta lay silent for a moment. "It's a thing my people had never heard of," he said quietly, "nor yours either, I suspect. As a boy I wanted to see the world, so I left home and traveled. I hired on a Danish ship as an oarsman. We went to Jötmark for lumber and took it to Frisland, where the cattle are fat but there are few trees. We took cattle to Britain then, where Anglic is the native tongue, and got the black stones that burn and took them to Frisland. There I jumped ship and walked south through the land of France, then through the land of Provence to the Southern Sea. In Provence, where there is no king, the lords are always at war with one another, and I took service with one as a mercenary. They use lots of mercenaries, and for that reason the language of their armies is Anglic.

"And in Provence I heard a legend that I believe has its roots in truth, of a magic jewel called the esper crystal. Looking into it, a man is supposed to be able to see and hear things far away or things that haven't happened yet. It's even said that the holder can read the thoughts of others through it."

Then Kuusta lay silent again.

"And what would you do with this crystal if you had it?" asked Nils.

"Get rich, I suppose."

"Have you thought how hard it would be to steal a thing as valuable as that from a person of great wealth and power when that person can see and hear things far away, look into the future, and maybe even read the thoughts of those around him?"

Kuusta lay quiet for some time, smelling the dead fire, but Nils knew he was not asleep. "Yes,"

Kuusta said finally, "I've thought about it. But I need something to strive for; otherwise, life would have no savor."

"And where do you think this esper crystal might be?"

"I don't know. The story is that once it was in a land east of the Southern Sea. But if it really exists, and if a person travels and watches and listens, he may learn where it is. Something like that must leave evidence."

"I'm not like you," Nils said. "I need nothing to strive for. You were right, in the inn. I'd have been happy to stay with my clan, hunting, raiding, fathering a line of warriors, and watching the seasons follow one another. Taking an arrow in my time or possibly growing old. But it's in my nature to do what is indicated, without worry or pain; so I am also happy to sleep in a Danish oak forest and travel I don't know where. I have no desire for this esper crystal or to get rich. But I'll travel with you for a while and learn from you."

Within a few moments Nils's breath slowed to the shallow cadence of sleep, and in Kuusta's mind the esper crystal shone like a cut gem glowing white, occupying his inner eye, until there was nothing else and he too was asleep.

The early light wakened them and they ate venison again. Kuusta visited his rabbit snares to no avail, while Nils dragged the deer carcass into a thicket. Each put a portion of roast haunch into his pack—enough to last until it would be too foul to eat—and they set off.

Soon they came out of the forest again, and the road was a lane between hedges atrill with birds.

Nils found the land pleasant. His eyes moved about, seeing things, interpreting, as he repeated the Anglic that Kuusta spoke for him.

He interpreted the rapid thudding of hooves, too, but the hedges at that point were a thick lacing of strong, thorny stems confining them to the lane until they could find a break. The horsemen came into sight quickly after the hoofbeats were heard, and Nils and Kuusta stood aside as they rode up, as if to let them pass. The five horsemen pulled up their mounts, however, and looked grimly down at the two travelers. Their green jerkins told Kuusta that these were game wardens of the local lord. Their leader, his knighthood marked by helmet and mail shirt, sat easily, sword drawn, smiling unpleasantly. Leaning forward, he reached a strong brown hand toward Kuusta.

"Your pack, rascal."

Kuusta handed up his pack, and the knight threw it to one of his men. Then he looked long and hard at Nils, who clearly was no ordinary wanderer. "And yours," he added.

Nils shrugged calmly out of his straps, took his shield off the pack, and handed the pack to the waiting hand. Kuusta tensed, suddenly convinced that Nils would jerk the man off his horse and they would die quickly by sword bite instead of slowly by noose. But Nils's hand released the pack and he stood relaxed. The men who opened the packs took out the roast meat and threw packs and venison into the dust of the lane. The knight licked his lips.

"Poachers. Do you know what we do with poachers?" he asked in slow Danish.

Poacher was a new word for Nils, although he took its meaning from context.

"What is a poacher?" he asked.

The knight and his green-clad men grinned. "A poacher is someone who kills the lord's deer," he explained. "Poachers are hung with their feet near the ground, and the dogs eat them."

"I have killed deer all my life," Nils said matter-of-factly. "Large deer called moose, and wild cattle, openly, and it has never been called a crime."

The knight studied Nils. His speech was strange and heavily accented; he was clearly a barbarian outlander of some sort. The knight had rarely seen foreigners before. The barbarian's sword, shield and steel cap were those of a man-at-arms, but his bare feet and torso were marks of a peasant. His manners were bolder than peasant manners, though. His size and brawn were those of a champion, but his young, unmarked face and scarless torso suggested green, unblooded youth.

"What are you?" the knight asked.

"A warrior."

"Of what wars?"

"Of no wars. Until this summer I was still a sword apprentice."

"Like a squire," Kuusta interpreted for the knight. "He is a Swede of the Svea tribe. There, ways are different than yours."

"Does your lord have use of fighting men?" Nils asked.

"If they are good."

"How does he test them?"

"They fight. With an experienced man-at-arms or a knight."

"Would he have use of two more?"

"I'm already of a mind to hang you from a tree as a warning to others who might have a taste for venison," the knight answered. "It is the custom here." He studied them further. "But with one as big as you it does seem a waste. It's possible you might fight well enough to serve his lordship. Certainly you're big enough, and bigger. If you can't, you can always serve as a thrall—or for public execution." He turned to one of his men. "Tie them," he ordered.

The man dismounted agilely with a long leather rope, and Nils and Kuusta submitted, wrists behind backs and loops around their necks. The horses trotted back down the lane then, in the direction they had been going, Nils and Kuusta running awkwardly behind, not daring to stumble. They were muddy with their own sweat and the dust kicked up by the horses, Kuusta cursing quietly but luridly in Finnish.

What kind of man is this Swede, Kuusta wondered? In town he seemed a great fighter, but here he had submitted as docilely as a thrall. Yet they *were* alive instead of stuck full of arrows like two porcupines. And the ropes around their necks had not been thrown over an oak limb.

They were put in a cell together in the barracks, but shortly a man-at-arms came and led them into the courtyard. A grizzled veteran stood there, with several other knights and squires, among them the knight who had brought them in.

The old knight glowered at the two prisoners. "So you claim to be fighting men," he said.

"I am a freeman of Suomi," said Kuusta. "I've served as a mercenary, and like all Suomalainet I am hightly skilled with the bow. In our country we live by the bow."

The veteran grunted. "Make him a mark," he ordered.

A squire picked up a horse dung and threw it thirty meters.

"Give him a bow."

Kuusta bent the unfamiliar bow, testing its flex and strength. "Can I use my own?" he asked. The old knight said nothing, so he fitted an arrow, drew back and let go. It struck centimeters short.

The old knight himself picked up a horse dung then and threw it high. Quickly Kuusta had to nock and draw, letting the arrow go when the target had already passed the height of the throw and was starting downward. The arrow broke it apart as it fell. Kuusta concealed his surprise.

The veteran tried not to look impressed. "Now you," he said to Nils, and signalled a man-at-arms who handed Nils his sword and shield. "And you, Jens Holgersen."

The knight who was game warden stepped out smiling, his sword drawn. He was not in the least awed by the size and musculature of the youth he faced—a half-naked barbarian of some tribe he'd never heard of. Besides, he had handled the opponent's sword and knew it was too heavy to be used properly, even by such a big ox. On top of that, the barbarian was barely past squiredom, unblooded and with no armor except his steel cap. Hopefully old Oskar Tunghand would stop it before the boy lay dead. Such size and strength could be trained if he didn't prove too clumsy, and besides, he'd taken a liking to the barbarian's open and honest disposition. He'd make a good Dane.

They faced each other. The boy showed no fear; his face was calm and his stance easy.

"Fight until I say to stop," the old knight ordered.

Their swords met with a crash, and Jens Holgersen began to hew. The youth parried, using sword as much as shield, and the knight was impressed at the ease with which he handled the heavy blade. He increased his efforts and the barbarian backed away, defending himself easily, measuring the strength and skill of the knight. Sword struck on sword and shield.

The man is not too bad, Nils decided, and with that he attacked. The great sword began to fly, smashing the other's sword back, the shocks jarring bone and sinew so that the knight could scarcely recover before the next blow struck. His shield was cloven nearly to the center with the blow that knocked him from his feet, and he lay in the dust, thunderstruck, the point of the heavy sword touching lightly at the latch of his throat.

"Must I kill him?" Nils asked casually, looking across at the old marshal. "He was merciful and spared our lives when he might have hanged us from a tree."

Oskar Tunghand stood erect, his brows knotted in consternation, his right hand on the hilt of his sword, not threateningly but in shock. "No, don't kill him. He"—the words almost choked the old knight—"is one of our best swordsmen."

Nils stepped back, put a foot on the encumbering shield and freed his sword. His wrist relaxed then, the point of his sword in the dust, and Jens Holgersen climbed slowly to his feet, his eyes on

the mild young face above him. He saw no exulta-
tion there, or even satisfaction. The eyes, squinting
against the sun, were simply thoughtful. And to
the astonishment of the watchers, when Holgersen
stood again, the young warrior knelt, picked up
the knight's fallen sword, handed it to him by the
hilt and slid his own back into the scabbard.

"Peder! Take them back to the barracks," Oskar
Tunghand said hoarsely. "See them fed and prop-
erly equipped." He turned to Jens Holgersen.
"Come."

Nils and Kuusta had walked several steps with
their guide when the old knight's rough voice called,
"Hey you, big one!" Nils stopped. "Your name."

"Nils Järnhann."

The veteran gazed at him for a moment. "Järnhann." His lips tightened slightly and he turned to
walk on with Jens Holgersen.

After Nils and Kuusta had washed and eaten, an
artificer attempted vainly to fit Nils from his exist-
ing supply of mail shirts. "I don't want one
anyway," Nils told him. "I'd feel ill at ease in it.
Among my people it's the custom for men to go
shirtless in warm weather. Would it offend your
customs if I go as I am?"

"It is the custom for knights to wear mail while
on duty, and Oskar Tunghand has ordered that
you be equipped as a knight. And it's the custom
of all but peasants to cover their bodies. It is strange
that you don't know these things. But as none of
these fit you, I'll have to make one that will.
Meanwhile, you'd better wear a shirt of some kind
or men will think you're uncouth and lowly."

Peder paa Kvernø, the man-at-arms in whose

charge they were, found a woolen shirt that Nils could wear. Then Nils found a sharpening steel and began to replace the edge on his sword.

The job was hardly well started when a page came to take him to an audience. They crossed the dusty courtyard and climbed a flight of stone stairs to enter the great hold, one pikeman preceding them and another following. The corridor was wide, with a tall door at the far end and lesser doors along both sides. The tall door was of thick oak, banded and bossed with iron and guarded by two pikemen. For all its weight it swung easily when the page pushed on it, and they entered a high, dim room richly hung with dark tapestries. Polished wood glowed in the light that came through narrow windows high in the walls and from oil lamps burning pungently in braziers.

A tall man with a great forked beard sat richly robed upon a throne. To one side stood Oskar Tunghand, with Jens Holgersen behind him in clean hose and jerkin. At his other side stood a white-bearded man, slight but erect in a blue velvet robe, his eyes intent on the newcomer. Behind the throne, on either side, stood a pikeman.

Nils walked down the carpeted aisle and was stopped five paces from the throne by a pike shaft.

The man on the throne spoke. "Has no one taught you to bow?"

"Bow?"

"Like this, dolt," said Tunghand, and he bowed toward the throne. Nils followed his example.

The slight, white-bearded man spoke next. "You are in the presence of his lordship Jørgen Stennaeve, Greve of Jylland, Uniter of the Danes and Scourge of the Frisians. Name yourself."

"I am Nils Järnhann, warrior of the Wolf Clan, of the Svea tribe."

The Greve of Jylland rose abruptly to his feet, his face darkening even in the poor light of the throne room. "Do you joke with me?" he demanded. "There cannot be an Iron Hand in the land of Stone Fist."

"Your lordship?" It was the soft, strong voice of white beard again.

"Yes?" snapped the greve.

"The names given by barbarians to barbarians need not concern us. Their names are conceived in ignorance of the world outside their forests and meant without harm to their betters." He turned and gestured toward Nils. "Look at him, your lordship. There is neither guile nor meanness there. Let him be called Nils Savage, for he is a barbarian, and let him serve you. I sense in him a service to your lordship that no one else can render."

Slowly the greve sat down again, and for a moment drummed his big fingers on the arm of his throne. "And you wish to serve me?" he asked at length.

"Yes, your lordship," Nils answered.

Jørgen Stennaeve turned to the white-bearded man. "We can't have a mere man-at-arms who can defeat our best knights; such a man should be instructed in manners and knighted. But I have never heard of knighting foreigners, and especially not barbarians. What do you say, Raadgiver?"

The white-bearded counselor smiled at Nils Järnhann. "What is your rank among your own people?"

"I am a warrior."

"And how did you come to be a warrior?"

"I was chosen in my thirteenth summer and trained for six years as a sword apprentice. Then my hair was braided and I was given my warrior name, and I became a warrior."

Raadgiver turned to the greve. "Your lordship," he said, "it seems that his people, in their barbaric way, have something rather like squires, which they call sword apprentices. And in due course they are made warriors, somewhat equivalent to knights, although uncouth. It is my thought that he need be called neither man-at-arms nor knight, but simply warrior. Let him live in the barracks with the men-at-arms, for he is a barbarian, but let him go into battle with the knights, for that is his training and skill."

At this construction, a smile actually played around the scarred lips of the grizzled Oskar Tunghand, and Jørgen Stennaeve, too, looked pleased. The greve rose again. "So be it," he said. "Let Nils Savage, barbarian, remain simply 'warrior,' housed with the men-at-arms but riding with the knights. What do you say to that, warrior?"

"Willingly, your lordship."

"Then return him to the barracks, Tunghand, and have him instructed in his duties."

5.

Outside, dim moonlight filtered through the overcast, but in the hut it was very dark. His senses strained for something, something he could not hear but faintly sensed. His scalp crawled. Dogs began to bark. And then there was a sound, a hooting that repeated—deep, toneless, directionless—and repeated again nearer. The barking became more shrill, then cut off, and a mindless terror that was not his but that he felt, a paralyzing terror, made them cower in their bed and pull the covers up so that they would not see what was coming for them. And the hooting was very near, in the lane outside, and he saw the door burst from the frame. Something huge and stooped filled the doorway, lurched toward the bed, and he yelled at the figures humped beneath the blankets and yelled. . . .

"Nils, wake up, wake up!" And Nils, trembling, clawed upright in bed, his heart pounding, eyes wild. "Wake up, you fool. You were roaring like a bear."

It was Kuusta, and other men-at-arms stood near, looking shocked and angry in their nightclothes.

"My blood, what a dream," Nils whispered. "What a dream." He sat clutching a twist of blanket in one huge fist, his breath deep and irregular. "What a terrible dream."

And for the rest of the night his sleep was troubled.

Surprisingly, when he awoke next morning, he could remember it clearly, although the terror was only an after-image, a shadow, remembered but no longer felt. Under Kuusta's coaxing he described it in the barracks, but by daylight it was not especially frightening. Peder paa Kvernø suggested that the fish at supper had seemed more overripe than usual.

Nils and Kuusta sat alone on a bench outside the barracks, digesting their breakfast of porridge and cheese. They talked in Anglic so far as Nils was able, which was considerable, for he grasped syntax almost instinctively, learned readily from context, and never forgot a word he had learned. And when he had trouble, Kuusta helped him. It was known that Jørgen Stennaeve planned to attack Slesvig, Denmark's southern province. Forces would be mustered from all his fiefs as soon as the harvest was over. If he forced the Greve of Slesvig to acknowledge his suzerainty, the Greve of Sjaelland would have to follow, and there would be a king again in Denmark.

"They don't prepare very seriously for war," Nils remarked. "At home each warrior has to make his living himself, yet he spends a lot more time practicing with weapons than most knights do. Sword apprentices in their sixteenth summer are more skilled than most knights. No wonder it was easy for me to beat one of their best. At home even freeholders have weapons and practice with birch swords, though more from tradition and in sport than from need. Almost everyone races and wrestles and shoots at marks, and everyone hunts. Children act out famous raids or make up their own. But here the knights and men-at-arms would rather drink or throw dice, and they don't practice with weapons nearly enough, most of them. Danes may be bold fighters, but they are not skilled fighters."

"They're as skilled as those I've seen in other lands," Kuusta replied. "I believe the big differences between these people and ours come partly from the land itself and partly from the laws. At home a man is his own master, to make a living or starve. In Suomi we do not even have thralls. There is all the land and all the game and a man can come and go as he pleases. He is free, and takes pleasure in contests. But in Suomi we don't have sword apprenticeship or a warrior class as your tribes do, and we make much less of raids and war."

"But there's another difference between the tribes and the Danes," Nils pointed out. "Here men can have only one wife, and the sons of knights become knights, while a thrall's son can only be a thrall unless he runs away to the free towns. At home a warrior can have three wives and many sons if he lives long enough. But his sons aren't necessarily chosen to become warriors, while the sons cf thralls are chosen fairly often. Our tradition calls it the law of positive selection. And our people increase; they have spread northward below the mountains as far as . . ."

Galloping hooves sounded from the drawbridge, and a constable on a lathered horse pounded through the gate and across the courtyard. Every eye followed him. He dropped from the saddle and ran up the stone steps of the great hold, speaking hurriedly to the guards, one of whom went in with him.

"I wonder what that's all about," Kuusta said, rising. They walked toward the hold in case anything might be overheard there.

"My dream," said Nils.

"Your dream? What do you mean?"

"It has to do with my dream."

"How could your . . . ? I don't understand."

"I dreamed of something that happened last night, kilometers away," Nils explained. "That one just brought the report of it."

Before the sun approached midday the troop of mounted men-at-arms were well away from the castle, under the command of a knight, with Nils as his second. They had been told only that a large and dangerous beast had killed some peasants in a village and that they were to destroy it.

They found the villagers in a state of shock. A family of four had been killed. It wasn't possible to determine how completely they had been eaten; remains had been scattered about with sickening ferocity, inside and out. But the fear among the villagers was out of proportion even to such savagery. Some were fitting stout bars on their doors; a few had fled to a nearby woods; still others only sat and waited for another night to come. The tracks of the beast had been obliterated in the lane through the village, but Nils and Kuusta were experienced trackers and found where the beast had struck the lane. They followed the trail on foot, leading their mounts, the troop following on horseback. Where the tracks crossed the soft ground of potato field, they got a clearer idea of what the animal was like. It walked upright on two oblong feet that were as long as Kuusta's forearm from elbow to knuckles. The toes were somewhat like a man's, but clawed.

"A troll!" said one of the men in an awed voice.

The knight spurred his horse up to the man and almost knocked him from the saddle with a fist blow. "There are no trolls," he snapped, "except in the stories grandfathers tell." The men sat sullenly. "Who has seen a troll?" he demanded. There was no answer. "Who has even heard of a troll except in fairy tales?"

One of the men laughed. "A troll! My grandmother used to tell me troll stories to make me mind." Other men began to smile or laugh.

But when they began to follow the trail again and saw the tracks pressed deeply into the hoed earth, they did not laugh anymore, or even talk.

"What do you think, Nils?" Kuusta asked quietly. "I haven't believed in trolls since I was a little boy. And in all my travels I have never seen or heard evidence of such a thing. But those!" He gestured toward the ground.

"These tracks and whatever made them are real," Nils answered. "If anyone wants to call it a troll, it's all the same to me."

The tracks entered a heath and became slow to follow, but they seemed to lead straight toward the sea. So Nils left Kuusta to trail through the low, dense shrubs, and mounting, he rode toward the sea with the knight. In less than three kilometers they came to the beach, and quickly found where the tracks crossed it and went into the water. Not twenty meters away they found where they had come out.

"There," said Nils, raising a thick sinewy arm. "That is its home." His big calloused forefinger pointed to a small island somewhat more than a kilometer offshore.

"How do you know?" asked the knight.

Nils shrugged.

The knight scowled across the quiet water. "You're probably right," he said. "And before we can get boats enough and go there, it'll be dark."

"If we start across, he might see us and escape anyway," Nils said. "Or it may be that he's good enough in the water to attack the boats from below. But he seems to like this place to leave and enter the water. Maybe we could lay behind the dune and ambush him."

The knight divided his troop. Half lay wrapped in their blankets back of the seaward dune, trying to sleep, while sentinels watched out to sea from behind clumps of dune grass that dotted the top. The other half, with the horses, took cover behind the next dune inland, ready to come in support if needed, or move parallel to the beach if the monster flanked the ambush.

With the ambush plans, the men began to feel more sure of themselves. The beast was big, no question of that, and savage. But most of them had been seasoned in combat and had confidence in themselves. And with bows, pikes and swords, they assured each other, they would make short work of it.

The moon was at the end of the third quarter and wouldn't rise until midnight. When the last light of dusk faded, the watchers could see little by the starlight. And the gentle washing of waves on the beach could cover the sound of anything emerging from the water.

"I don't like this darkness," the knight muttered softly.

"I don't think he'll come until after the moon rises," Nils answered in a whisper. "Last night the moon was well up before he entered the village. He probably likes more light than this himself."

"How do you know the moon was well up?"

"Because, looking through the window, I could see the moonlight."

"Oh yes, I heard about your dream," the knight said. "The story has gone around the castle." He turned to Nils, staring at him in the darkness, then looked back out to sea. Dimly he could distinguish the dark water from the lighter beach. "I don't believe in dreams," he added.

In spite of themselves they dozed now and then. Suddenly Nils jerked wide-awake, startling the knight beside him. The half-moon stood above the rim of the sea and the night was light, but it wasn't that that had wakened him. The beast was coming, in the water, with a hunger for flesh and for more than flesh, for the current of life, spiced with terror, was nourishment as necessary to it as food. And Nils was in its avid mind, feeling with its senses. It felt the buoyancy and resistance and coolness of the water as it watched the dunes not far ahead. And it sensed that among the dunes was what it sought.

Nils shook his head and looked about him with his own eyes again. "He's coming," he whispered softly. "And he knows we're here."

The knight said nothing, but rose to one elbow and stared out to sea.

"It's not in sight yet," Nils told him, "but it will be soon." He slid down the back side of the dune and began waking the sleepers one-by-one with a touch and a whisper. They rolled out of their blankets, awake and taut, and followed Nils to the crest.

Nils sensed the knight's rigidity and looked seaward. The beast could be seen now, twenty or thirty meters from the shore, wading slowly in the shallow water. It looked immense, perhaps two-and-a-half meters tall, its proportions resembling those of an overgrown gorilla except that it was longer legged. But its hide, wet and moonlit, looked like chain mail.

It stopped for a moment where the waves washed onto the beach, turned briefly to look over its shoulder at the moon, then scanned the dune as if it could see them. An overanxious bowman loosed an arrow, and a hail of others hissed after it to fall from the beast's hide onto the sand. For just an instant it stood, shielding its face with a massive forearm. Then a line of shouting men charged from the crest, brandishing pikes and swords.

A hoarse hoot came from the beast, and something else. A great wave of something. Men staggered, dropped their weapons, and war cries changed to howls and shrieks of mindless terror.

Some ran, stumbling, rising, back up the dune or along the beach or into the sea. Others simply fell, wrapping their arms around their heads in catatonic helplessness.

Nils felt the waves of terror as on the night before, terror that was not his own but that shook him momentarily. The few arrows that had stuck in the beast dangled as if only the points had penetrated. He picked up a pike and charged down the dune again, the only one now, bulging arms cocked, and at three meters lunged with all his strength at the towering monster, his hands near the butt of the pike, and felt the head strike and break through. His follow-through carried him rolling onto the sand, diagonally and almost into the legs of the beast, the hilt of his scabbarded sword striking him painfully below the ribs. He rolled to his feet, stumbling as the beast rushed at him, bulky but quick, the pike shaft sticking out of its belly. There was only time to grab the shaft before the beast was on him.

The charge threw Nils backward, off his feet, sliding on his back across the sand, his grip like iron on the shaft, his arms and shoulders tensed with all their strength. Great clawed fingers clutched short of him, and the hoot changed to a roar of rage and pain as the beast dropped to its knees. When the pike had pierced its entrails it had been like fire bursting into it. But the collision, with the man grabbing the shaft, and the shock as he had hit the ground, transmitted through two-and-a-half meters of strong ash, did terrible damage.

Nils let go and rolled sideways to his feet, drawing his sword as the beast rose again. It wrenched the pike from its own guts, eyes raging, and charged once more. The sword struck once, into the rib cage, and they crashed to the ground together. One great forearm pressed down on Nils's throat and he grabbed desperately at the scaly neck, straining to keep its fangs from him. His last thought, fading but distinct, was that its blood smelled like any other.

6.

Consciousness came gradually. First Nils was aware of his body, then of voices. After a bit he focused on the voices, and their Anglic began to take meaning.

"So we have a psi who is also deadly," a female voice was saying. "But why does it have to be a filthy, ignorant barbarian?"

Nils opened his eyes.

Raadgiver, in his blue velvet robe, sat beside the cot looking down at Nils and smiling slightly. A young woman, taller than the counselor, stood at the window looking out, her black hair in a braid down her slender back.

"Signe, our patient is awake," Raadgiver said in Danish. He pulled on a velvet cord and somewhere a bell rang. Signe turned. She was not much more than a girl—perhaps no older than Nils—and handsome, but her startling blue eyes bespoke dislike.

"Nils Savage, this is my daughter and apprentice. I need not introduce you to her, for she has shared the job of watching over you since you were brought to the castle earlier this morning. I have been your other nurse."

Nils sat up on the edge of the cot thoughtfully. He wore only his breeches; his other things lay on a nearby bench. "I don't seem to be injured, only weak," he said. "The troll must have died almost as soon as I lost consciousness."

"Troll!" said Signe, turning to her father without trying to hide her scorn of such superstition.

"Do you believe it was a troll, Nils?" asked Raadgiver.

"Not in the sense of the fairy tales," he answered. "But it's useful to have a name to call it. It's not an animal from this part of the world; if it was, we'd know about it, and not by grandfathers' tales but by its deeds and attributes.

"Brave men who saw it and what it had done weren't terrified by the sight. They believed they could kill it. But when it howled, they were filled with terror, and their minds were like eyes that had looked at the sun. And it wasn't the howl that did it, really, at least not by itself. If I made the same sound, no one would panic."

Nils looked calmly up from his seat on the cot. "And I could see through its eyes, and knew it was coming before it was seen or heard."

"Why didn't you panic?" Raadgiver asked. "You were the only one who didn't, you know. Did you feel no fear?"

"I felt the fear all right," Nils replied. "But it wasn't my own. I think that somehow it was from the others as well as from the troll. It was like a wave washing over me without wetting me."

There was a rap on the heavy door of the chamber, and Raadgiver spoke. A servant entered and left a platter with a steaming roast, mushrooms, a loaf, and a large mug.

"Well," Raadgiver said, "we'll leave you with this, for we have eaten and will return when you've finished." He held the door for Signe, at the same time turning again to Nils. "Do you speak Anglic, Nils?" he asked.

"Some," Nils answered. "I've been learning it for several weeks."

Raadgiver almost grinned for a moment, and nudged his daughter as the door closed behind them. "I believe your 'filthy, ignorant barbarian' heard and understood that little remark just before he opened his eyes," he thought to her. "And what do you think of him now, my dear? He is hardly more than a boy, a very large boy, but he has a mind like a razor."

Signe's answer was a flash of irritation.

Nils chewed the end of the loaf, which held all that was left of the gravy, then tipped the last of the ale from the mug and wiped his mouth on the back of a thick hand. Standing, he pulled the bell cord and walked to the narrow window. The thick stone walls restricted the viewing angle, but the room was high and he could see over the castle wall. The patchwork of fields and woods, so different from the endless forests, bogs and lakes of Svealann, lay peaceful and warm in the sunshine of an August afternoon.

He did not turn when a servant entered and took out the platter. A moment later, Raadgiver and Signe returned.

Without preliminaries, Nils asked, "What is it you want me to do?"

"Why do you think we want you to do anything?" Raadgiver countered.

Nils, leaning casually against the wall, said nothing, simply folding his muscular arms across his chest.

Raadgiver laughed suddenly and addressed his daughter out loud. "My dear, this would be the man we need, even if he wasn't a psi. If I praise him, he won't be embarrassed because he'll know it's merely the truth. And if you insult him, he won't be irritated because it won't matter to him, being untrue.

"And besides, I can't read his thoughts except when he speaks."

Raadgiver lowered himself into a cushioned chair and looked up at Nils more seriously now. "Do you know the word 'psi'?"

"No."

"Psi is the ability to read minds, to converse silently or to look into the future. Very few can do these things. Small children with the potential to learn aren't rare, but in most cases the potential is lost if it isn't developed by the fourth or fifth year. Among the occasional adults who retain it, it is almost always erratic and usually weak, unless trained."

"I've had that sort of experience only twice," Nils said. "In my dream two nights ago, when my mind was in the peasant hut, and last night, when the troll was swimming from the island."

"Only twice strongly," Raadgiver corrected, "but perhaps many other times less obviously. I read the minds of those who were at your audience with the greve. You had handed Jens Holgersen his sword after beating him, and then you sheathed your own. Wasn't that reckless? He could easily have

killed you then, and many men would have. Yet
bravado and foolishness are as foreign to your
nature as weakness is."

"I knew he wouldn't," said Nils.

"Good. But how could you be so sure? You hardly
knew him," Raadgiver pointed out. "When we say
that an untrained psi shows erratic ability, we
refer to conscious psi experience. Most such people,
or probably all, receive many other psi impressions unconsciously—that is, psi messages enter
their minds, but they don't recognize them for
what they are. But the information is in their minds
anyway. That is—" He paused. "It's very hard to
explain to someone who has no concept of the
subconscious mind."

"I understand you," Nils said.

Raadgiver leaned back in his chair, his intensity
suddenly gone. "Of course," he said. "You would."

"And now, back to my question," Nils reminded
him.

"Ah yes. What we want you to do. We're working up to that." Raadgiver shifted in his seat, looking tired now and no longer meeting Nils's eyes.
He spoke quietly. "What is the most important
thing to a man next to life itself?"

"For many, what he really believes is true."

Raadgiver stared up for a moment, then looked
down at his nails. "Only if he isn't suffering. If he's
suffering enough, the most important thing is for
the suffering to stop. It can be more important
than survival. And if he lives in constant fear—fear
of terrible pain, of the real and imminent threat of
physical and mental torture—then the most important thing becomes freedom from that threat."

Nils had never heard of such a situation.

"Now suppose there was a land where all men were thralls. No, less than thralls, because thralls at least have some rights and protection in law. Suppose all men were slaves except for one master and his soldiers. And suppose that master had the worst kind of madness, finding his greatest pleasure in the misery and degradation, the torture, of his slaves. An emperor who conquered only to enjoy the cries, the whimpers, the begging for mercy of those he ruled. A man who had lived very long and has a great army." Raadgiver leaned toward Nils. "What would you do if you lived in a land like that?"

"I have never thought of such a thing," Nils answered. "It would depend on the possibilities."

"But suppose that lord offered to make you his lieutenant?" Raadgiver asked.

"The lieutenant would still be his thrall. Where is that land?"

"Right now it is far to the southeast," Raadgiver answered. "But someday, perhaps soon, it may include all of Europe, even Denmark.

"And what we want you to do is kill that man."

7.

Jørgen Stennaeve was tough, ambitious, and direct, but not particularly intelligent. Given cause for distrust, he could be suspicious and wary, but otherwise he tended to take things at face value and was also disinterested in details other than military. So when his chief counselor asked for charge of the barbarian, he asked few questions. Raadgiver simply explained that he believed the troll was sent by an evil power in a distant land. That evil power hoped someday to spread into Europe, perhaps even to Denmark. Nils withstood the troll because of a certain strength against that power, he went on, and Raadgiver wanted to train him and send him to fight it.

To the greve the menace seemed remote and the value of such a fighting man might be considerable in the impending invasion of Slesvig. But, on the other hand, the counselor's advice was almost always good, so he agreed to the request. Thus, Nils moved from the barracks to a small chamber near the apartment of Raadgiver and Signe, and began his lessons. Raadgiver instructed him, or Signe, when her father was otherwise occupied.

Most psi experiences are telepathy, Nils was told. Psis can read thoughts only when there are explicit thoughts to read—that is, when the mind is discursive—and psi conversation consists primarily of thinking words, feelings and pictures to one another. When the attention is on some sensory experience, that experience too can be shared, as when Nils looked at the beach through the troll's eyes and felt the water with its body.

Emotional states, including the finer nuances, are easily sensed, and a psi commonly receives a general but appropriate reading of overall personality at first encounter.

Psionic transmissions normally are subject to the inverse square law, but can be received at something beyond normal hearing distance when transmitted forcefully or in a psychically quiet environment. With training, the potentially psi-receptive mind reflexively develops selective damping, providing a large degree of protection against "psi noise." Damping can be cut selectively for screening transmissions, as for seeking one particular mind in a crowd. And when that mind is found, the attention can be focused on it while reception of others remains damped.

Damping is not very effective against transmissions directed specifically toward the receiver, however.

Unexplainable exceptions occur to the inverse square limitation. Occasional transmissions carry thousands of kilometers without apparent weakening. These are highly specific to a receiver or receivers, and the receiver need not be a trained psi. Little is known about this phenomenon and such transmissions cannot be made at will. They are, therefore, of little importance.

There is also a technological exception to the inverse square restriction. Before the Great Death, an instrument called a psi tuner was invented, permitting the narrow focusing of telepathic transmissions to another psi tuner. They are useful only to trained psis.

Precognition and premonition are the other known facets of psi. In the untrained psi these commonly are in the form of symbolic visions, but among trained psis they are usually explicit previews having the same quality and much of the impact of a sensory perception. Premonitions are not necessarily fulfilled, falling into the category of "what will happen if nothing intercedes." Precognition, on the other hand, seems to fall into the category of "what will happen regardless." Many trained psis state they can distinguish them. A strong philosophical case has been made, however, for the contention that there is no precognition in that strict sense, the difference between the experiences lying in the degree of probability that they will be fulfilled.

Premonition and precognition cannot be experienced at will. They occur rarely or possibly never at all to some psis, infrequently to most, and somewhat frequently to a few. Commonly occurring without context, the receiver often cannot understand what he "saw," and the event foreseen may be important or irrelevant to him.

Raadgiver also described the loose organization of psis that had grown up in Europe.

"In the year 2105 there were five billion people

on Earth," he said. "Can you imagine that, Nils? That is a thousand taken a thousand times. And then that thousand thousand taken a thousand times again, and five times all of those. It is beyond comprehension. Single towns had more people than probably exist in all the world today. That is our tradition in the Psi Alliance. And then the Great Death came, and within a few weeks so many had died that a man could walk for days before he saw another living person.

"The ancients had great learning and made much use of machines. Machines pumped water into every dwelling through metal tubes, even to the tops of towers. People rode in flying boats faster than the fastest arrows. They even rode them to the stars, which are other worlds like this one. Subtle machines did their labor, drawing power from beams like sunlight but invisible and akin to lightning. But each machine needed men with special skills to take care of it, and it had to be told what to do. So when their keepers died, the machines became confused and soon they too began to die. And when the machines died that made the power, almost all the others died at once.

"And the people with the plague were seized with the desire to set fires, as a man with a cold must cough or sneeze. The few who survived inherited a smoking ruin.

"At first, they hoped that those who'd gone to the stars would come back someday and bring the machines back to life. But they never did, and it's probable that the plague struck them, too.

"One who survived was a trained psi named Jakob Tashi Norbu, who taught in a great place of learning called the University of Lucerne. In those days there was a powder that could be given to a person to tell whether or not he had psi potential, and he searched on foot through Europe, after the Death, looking for psis. He found three. He also searched the places of learning for psi tuners and found thirteen. Mine is one of them.

"It took him years.

"Father Jakob taught each of his psis and gave them tuners. They took mates and most of the children were psis. That was the beginning of the Alliance.

"Over the generations men's numbers increased, and lords and chiefs appeared. So the Alliance dispersed; it was becoming unsafe to be a separate community. Fourteen had psi tuners, and these worked themselves into the service of lords and chiefs as advisors. They kept their talents secret and used them to advance good lords or cause the fall of bad. Within the Alliance, those with psi tuners are called the Inner Circle. Over the centuries the Inner Circle has had an important influence on the ascension and the acts of rulers.

"Some without tuners also are advisors, and in most important towns there is at least one free merchant who is a psi. These we call the Kinfolk; some of us refer to the whole Alliance as the Kinfolk. And they, too, keep their talents a secret.

"Still others have become wanderers. We call them the Wandering Kin, but the peasants call them the Brethren. They wander through the countryside and among the villages as storytellers, teachers and magicians, speaking Anglic almost exclusively. This helps keep Anglic alive so that men of different lands can speak with each other. They awe the people by knowing their secrets and use their skills to seem supernatural. When available, the peasants call upon them to judge disputes. Their stories become traditions and their acts legends, and so far as their understanding and ability allows, they try to reduce the cruelty and injustice that men perpetrate on men.

"The Wandering Kin have their own tradition. They own nothing but the clothes they wear and a sleeping robe for when they must spend the night beside the road. The peasants feed and shelter them and give them clothes, regarding it a privilege. Only in unpeopled stretches do the Wandering Kin own even a hut, built by themselves in the wilderness, where they can shelter in bad weather."

Raadgiver also taught him how psis influence the thinking of non-psis. A psi cannot influence a subject to a conclusion or action incompatible with the subject's nature. But his reaction to a specific idea or event commonly can be modified. For example, the influence of a psi advisor on his feudal lord depends on:

1. Selection of a lord who is not particularly suspicious of him or adverse to advice, followed by the cultivation of the lord's confidence.

2. Sound insight into the lord's personality. An important element in psi training is training to interpret thoughts and emotions and to integrate them into a reasonable model of the subject's subconscious so his reactions can be predicted.

3. Correct reading of the lord's mood of the moment, which is automatic for a trained psi.

4. Ability to translate the psi's objective, or an approximation of it, into an objective harmonic

with the lord's tastes or at least compatible with them.

Nils also was instructed in geography, map reading, and use of the psi tuner. Raadgiver also passed on odd bits and pieces of subjects from geology to philosophy. As far as possible, instruction and conversation were in Anglic.

The man Nils was to assassinate was a psi named Kazi. The Alliance had first become aware of him several decades earlier as the ruler of a powerful Near Eastern despotism. One of the Kinfolk equipped with a psi tuner had been sent to spy on him and was captured. Apparently he succeeded in suicide, however, for Kazi seemed to have gotten little information from him. But he clearly deduced the existence of a European psi organization. For a time Kazi had sent psi spies of his own into Europe, losing several but assassinating three of the Inner Circle. Apparently he concluded that so loose and nonmilitary an organization as the Alliance was no threat to him, for no more spies had been detected for a number of years.

Meanwhile, Kazi had expanded his empire to include much of the Balkans.

Reports and rumors gathered by the Wandering Kin in peripheral areas and from refugees indicated that Kazi's rule was one of deliberate depravity, and that he was clearly psychopathic. His subjects lived in a pathetic state of fear or apathy, and his army was thought to be invincible.

Legends described him as the Never Dying. Evidence indicated that he actually was either ageless, extremely old, or more probably a dynasty.

Apparently he intended to conquer Europe. He

had planted a cult to Baalzebub throughout much
of the continent, Baalzebub referring to himself.
Under the influence of drugs, initiates practiced
such obscene depravities that they felt themselves
afterward totally alienated from their culture and
either dedicated themselves completely to the cult
or committed suicide.

It had few adherents now, however. Initiates
were easily detected by the Kinfolk, and using the
information they provided, the feudal lords had
suppressed the cult harshly. And the Wandering
Kin preached against it.

Recently trolls had appeared along the coasts of
western and northern Europe, and the rumor had
been spread that Baalzebub had sent them because the people did not worship him.

The Alliance had been looking for someone
who might stand a chance of assassinating Kazi.
Raadgiver told Nils frankly that success seemed
less than likely, and that Kazi could well come to
rule all of Europe.

Nils left the castle in the dry haze of an October
day, alone.

"After two months you still dislike him, Signe,"
Raadgiver thought. "Shall I tell you why?"

"He has no sensitivities," Signe answered aloud.

Raadgiver continued as if she hadn't spoken.
"Because he doesn't think as we do nor feel the
same emotions. I sensed that in him when I first
saw him, at his audience with the greve. He didn't
think discursively except when he spoke. His mind
receives, correlates and decides, but it does not
'think to itself.'

"Because of that difference you dislike him; yet

if we weren't so different ourselves, we wouldn't know it. Everyone else at the castle likes him because he is so mild and pleasant.

"Signe, we are told that before the Great Death, when psi was not secret, many people disliked or even hated psis. And not because of the ways they acted or the things they said, but because psis were so different and, in a way, superior.

"Nils is still another kind of human, different and, in an important way, superior to us. It bothers you to hear me say it, yet you sensed that superiority at once, and watched it grow.

"Yet we have our part in it, for without us it would not have matured. His mind was impressive from the first, but its scope has broadened and deepened greatly during his weeks with us, and as he absorbs experiences through psi. . . ."

Signe's thought interrupted his angrily. "And he isn't even grateful!" she flared.

"True. He knows what happened, what we did, and accepts it as a matter of fact. That's his nature. And it seems to be yours to dislike him for it. But remember this while you're enjoying the questionable pleasure of indignation. At our request he is going to probable death without question or hesitation. And who else would have a significant chance of success?"

8.

During his training under Raadgiver, Nils worked out for a time each morning, mostly giving Kuusta lessons in the use of sword and shield. The Finn already knew the basics and was strong for his size. Also, he had grown up in a relentless wilderness environment, as a hunter, with hunger or a full belly as the stakes. His senses were sharp and his reflexes excellent. By late September Kuusta had more than thickened in the arms and shoulders; he had become one of the best swordsmen among the men-at-arms, and afoot could have held his own against some of the knights.

Generally, however, the life of a man-at-arms had palled on Kuusta Suomalainen. First, it was dull. Under the gentle influence of his chief counselor, the Greve of Slesvig had been sufficiently impressed by the mobilization of Jylland forces to offer homage to Jørgen Stennaeve as King of Denmark. So there was no war. Second, Kuusta was homesick. He had compared the wide world with his memories of Finland and was beginning to find the wide world lacking.

Jens Holgersen had appreciated his woods cunning and assigned him to night patrol for poachers, which had been pleasant enough until the evening they had caught a peasant with a deer.

His main satisfaction was in training with Nils, sweating, aching, feeling the growth of skill and strength. So when Nils told him that he soon would be leaving, alone, Kuusta also began to think about leaving, and with Raadgiver's influence he was released from his service.

On the evening before Kuusta was to leave, he sat with Nils outside the castle, by the moat. "Why have you decided to go home instead of searching for the esper crystal?" Nils asked. He knew Kuusta's mind, but asked by way of conversation.

"The esper crystal?" Kuusta grunted. "It seemed real and desirable enough to me once, but now I'd rather see Suomi again. I want to hunt, sweat in the sauna, and speak my own language in a land where men are not hanged up with their eyes bulging and their tongue swelling while they slowly choke to death. And all because they wanted some meat with their porridge."

"And how will you get there?" Nils asked.

"I've seen a map showing that if I ride eastward far enough, I'll come to the end of the sea, and if I go around the end, I'll come to Suomi."

"And do you know what the people are like in the lands you'll pass through?"

Kuusta shrugged. "Like the people in most lands, I suppose. But being obviously poor and riding a horse somewhat past his prime, I won't be overly tempting to them. And since you've treated me so mercilessly on the drill ground, I'll be less susceptible to them. Actually, if the truth was known, I'm leaving to escape those morning sessions with you, but I wouldn't tell you that straight-out because even the ignorant have feelings."

"It's nice to have a friend so thoughtful of me," Nils responded. "We fully grown people are as sensitive as you midgets."

Kuusta aimed a fist to miss the blond head next to him, and Nils dodged exaggeratedly, rolling away to one side. Then they got up, went back into the castle, and shook hands in parting.

Early the next morning Kuusta Suomalainen rode across the drawbridge on the aging horse his soldier's pay had bought him, with a sword at his side, a small saddle bag tied behind him, and a safe-pass signed by Oskar Tunghand.

It was an October day on a forested plain in northern Poland, sunny but cool, with a fair breeze rattling the yellow leaves in the aspens and sending flurries of them fluttering down to carpet the narrow road. But Kuusta was not enjoying the beauty. Periodically he broke into coughing that bent him over the horse's withers and left him so weak he didn't see the man standing in the road facing him until the horse drew up nervously. The man wore a cowled jacket of faded dark-green homespun and carried a staff over one shoulder. His face approached the brown of a ripe horse chestnut, darker than the shock of light brown hair that looked to have been cut under a bowl.

"Good morning," the man said cheerfully in Anglic. "You sound terrible."

Kuusta looked at him, too sick to be surprised at having been greeted in other than Polish.

"Where are you going in such poor shape?" the man asked.

"To Finland," Kuusta answered dully.

"Let me put it another way," the man said. "Where are you going today? Because wherever it is, unless it's very nearby, you'll never make it. I've just come from a shelter of the Brethren very near here, and if you're willing, I'll take you there." He paused. "My name is Brother Jozef."

Kuusta simply nodded acquiescence while staring at the horse's neck.

The shelter was out of sight of the road, the path leading there being marked by a cross hacked in the bark of a roadside pine. It was built of un-squared logs chinked with clay, and had two rooms, a small one for occupancy and a smaller one for storage and dry firewood.

Jozef helped Kuusta from the horse and through the door. Inside it was dark, for he had closed the shutters earlier before leaving, but he knew his way around and led Kuusta to a shelflike bed with a grass-filled ticking on it, built against the wall. Then he disappeared outside. As Kuusta's eyes adjusted to the gloom, he raised himself on one elbow to look around. A fit of coughing seized him, deep and painful, and he fell back gasping. He began to shiver violently, and when Jozef came back in, he put down his armload of firewood and covered Kuusta with the sleeping robe from the saddlebag and then with another ticking from the storeroom.

In the night Kuusta's moans wakened the Pole. The Finn's body tossed and twisted feverishly in the darkness, his mind watching a battle. Jozef could see hundreds of knights on a prairie, fleeing in broken groups toward a forest. Pursuing them was a horde of wild horsemen wearing mail shirts and black pigtails, cutting down stragglers. Then a phalanx of knights appeared from the forest, led by the banner of Casimir, King of Poland. They launched themselves at the strung-out body of pig-tailed horsemen, who abandoned their pursuit and tried to form themselves against the challenge. In moments the charging knights struck, sweeping many of them away, and they broke into groups of battling horsemen, chopping and sweating and dying on the grassland.

Kuusta sat up with a hoarse cry, and the scene was gone. Slowly he lay back, his mind settling again into feverish sleep, only ripples and twitches remaining of the violent disturbance of a moment before.

But Brother Jozef sat awake, staring unseeingly at the glow that showed through the joints of the box stove. To his trained psi mind, the difference between the pickup of a dream and that of a quasi-optical premonition was definite and unmistakable. This traveler was an undeveloped psi.

9.

The weather had been almost continuously pleasant during Nil's journey, but on this late October day the sky was threatening. Earlier in the morning he had left a broad valley of farms and small woods for wild rocky hills, following a canyon that narrowed to pinch the road between steep, fir-clad slopes.

The first pickup he had of the ambush was the faint mental response of the robbers when they heard his horses's hooves clop over a cobbly stretch where the brook turned across the road.

He stopped for a brief moment. There seemed to be five of them, perhaps seventy or eighty meters ahead, but they couldn't see him yet. He slid from the saddle with bow, sword and shield, slapped the horse on the rump, and moved into the thick forest, slipping quietly along the slope above the road while the horse jogged toward the ambush.

He heard shouts ahead and moved on until, through a screen of trees, he could see what had happened. Apparently the horse had shied and tried to avoid capture, for they had shot it and were tying his gear onto one of the three horses that the five of them shared. Quickly he drew his bow and shot an arrow, and another, and another, two of the robbers falling while the other three scrambled onto the horses and galloped away. His third arrow had glanced from a sapling branch.

His horse lay still alive, four arrows in its body. He knelt beside the outstretched neck, cut its throat, and caught his steel cap full of the gushing blood. After he had had his fill, he washed the cap in the brook.

Then he searched the bodies. It was clear that robbers were not prospering in Bavaria. These two didn't even have the flint and steel he was looking for. He cut a long strip of flesh from his horse's flank, put it inside his jacket, and started walking down the road. A few big, wet snowflakes started to drift down. In less than half a kilometer they were falling so thickly that the ground's warmth couldn't melt them as fast as they landed, and it began to whiten. Within a kilometer visibility had dropped to a few score meters. The temperature was falling too, and soon the snow was no longer wet and sticky. By the time Nils had crossed a low pass and started into the next forested canyon, the snow was almost halfway to his knees.

These wild hills were extensive, and not a narrow range between two settled districts; by late afternoon he still had not come to shelter. The snow was thigh-deep and showed no sign of slowing, while the temperature still was edging downward. Under the denser groves of old firs the snow was much less deep, piling thickly on the branches. His sword striking rapidly, Nils cut a number of shaggy fir saplings and dragged them under a dense group of veterans, building a ridge-roofed shelter hardly waist-high. Next he stripped a number of others, stuffing the shelter almost full of their boughs and piling more at the entrance. Then, with his shield, he threw a thick layer of snow over it. Finally he burrowed into the bough-filled interior feet first, stuffed the entrance full of boughs in front of him, and soon was dozing, chilled and fitful.

By dark the entrance, too, was buried under snow.

Through the night he was dimly aware of time and of being cold, never deeply asleep, never wide awake. Later he was aware of dim light diffusing through the snow, marking the coming of day, but with the instinct of a boar bear he knew it still was storming. Twice he wakened enough to eat some of the raw horsemeat, and later he knew that darkness had returned, and still later that again it was daylight.

Nils sensed now that the storm was over, and he was stiff with cold. Burrowing out of the shelter, he stood erect. The snow was chest-deep under the old firs and deeper elsewhere. The sky was clear and the hairs of his nostrils stiffened at once with the frost. With his sword he cut two fir saplings, trimmed them on two sides and, with fingers clumsy from cold, tied them to his boots with leather strips from his jacket. On these makeshift snowshoes he started up the road again.

Moisture from his breath formed frost beads on his lashes and caked his fledgling mustache and beard. Although it was awkward, he walked with his gloveless hands inside his jacket, his fingers under his arms. His thighs soon ached with cold.

He was dressed only for a raw autumn day, not for an arctic air mass.

Hours passed, hours that would have killed most men.

Nils felt the cold as a physical-physiological phenomenon and knew that after a time it would damage his body severely, even lethally, if he did not find shelter soon enough. The cold would be much less severe if he sheltered under the snow again, but the constant chill would deplete his remaining energy reserves without bringing him nearer to safety. Dressed as he was, to hole up again might delay death, but it would also assure it.

With each step he had to raise his feet high to clear the clumsy snowshoes from the deep, fluffy snow, and as the kilometers passed, his strides became gradually slower and shorter. His feet were like wood despite the exertion, his hands numb and useless, and his body had stopped feeling the cold. The sun had set, and he crossed another ridge in growing darkness. He was not consciously aware of it when night fell.

Suddenly he became alert, smelling faint smoke, sensing the direction of the air movement. Moving slowly, he turned from the road, plowing a deep furrow as he went. Dimly he sensed a mind, felt it sense his.

The hut was half a kilometer from the road—a hump in the snow with the door partly cleared. Other eyes saw the door through his, and as he dragged toward it, it opened. A tall woman stepped out with a long knife, cut the snowshoes from his feet, and helped him inside.

*   *   *

Nils awoke rested and utterly famished. The woman turned to him, pulled back the covers and let him look at himself through her eyes. He knew his hands and feet should have been swollen and split and painful, but they weren't. The skin was peeling from them, and from his face and the front of his thighs, but they didn't seem really damaged.

"My name is Nils," he thought to her. "What is yours?"

"Ilse," she answered, adding, "you have been here three nights and two days."

"How did you do it?" he asked, thinking of the hands and feet that should have been in much worse condition and might well have been gangrenous.

"Through your sleeping mind."

"How?"

"I spoke to it, leading it, and your mind led your flesh to make new flesh in the layers that were dying. My father taught me how."

Ilse's father had been one of the merchant Kinfolk, she explained, and had sensed power in himself that the Kinfolk did not know about. So he had taken his wife and small daughter into the quiet of the wilderness to meditate and explore himself, while his eldest son took his place as a merchant and subtle force in the free town of Neudorf am Donau. Another son had joined the Wandering Kin.

Ilse had grown up in the forest curious and aware, free of the psi static that most psi children grew up with in towns. So she sensed the minds of animals. In most of them there was little enough to read—anxiety, desire, curiosity, anger, comfort and discomfort, all transient. It was a background to her days, like the breeze in the tree tops.

"And then," she thought to Nils, "one day I

reached out and touched the mind of an old he-wolf, and he felt the touch. For in these hills the wolves have psi. If one is born without it, they kill it so that it will not suffer the handicap. They confer silently, using their voices only as an accompaniment. Next to man they are by far the most intelligent animals in the hills, and they compensate for the still narrow limits of their minds by their rationality and their psi.

"They experience emotions, in a sense, but the emotion simply happens, without building on itself. They feel fondness but never sentiment. When a wolf fears, it is a fear of something real and present, a response to an immediate danger, and he looks at it as he looks at hunger or a tree or a rabbit. It is there, and he acts accordingly, without confusion." Ilse looked at Nils in the dim light filtering through the scraped deerskins stretched over the windows. "In many ways," she added slowly, "the minds of wolves are like yours.

"I am the first human the wolves had ever shared minds with, at least in this forest, and we have done so many times. We communicate by mind pictures, to which we give emotional content when we want to, and we've developed considerable subtlety. It's pleasant for them, and for me, too. Through them I have run through the snow with starlight glittering it, and I've felt their joy in a warm scent. From me they sense new ideas, unthought-of concepts, and while they understand them only vaguely, it gives them a sense of mind-filling, like the feeling they get when they look at a clear night sky and sense a universe beyond understanding.

"So I've always been safe when wolves are about,

and if possible they would protect me if I was threatened."

Ilse rose from the bench and took furs from a box—clothing and a sleeping bag, all large. "These are yours when you leave. Your skis are outside."

Nils's mind questioned.

"Yes, I had a premonition a year ago. After a great storm you woud come here, unless you were killed earlier. You would come here weak and frozen and unequipped for winter. And there was more. You will go to the great town called Pest and serve Janos, King of the Magyars."

Nils stayed with Ilse for several days, resting and learning.

10.

During the days since he had left Ilse the arctic cold had eased a great deal, but winter still held strong. The snow had settled some, but there had been no thawing. He had passed through inhabited districts again. Peasants were out on skis, with their oxen and sleighs, hauling firewood or the bodies of cattle that had died in the storm. In Anglic they told him glumly that the surviving cattle would be on short rations by spring, for they were usually able to forage in the woods until near the solstice, but now they were eating their hay already. And the cold they had had was rare even in the middle of winter.

Nils still had some Danish coins in his money belt and twice stayed at inns, where he was warned that the Magyars did not like foreigners, that most of them did not speak Anglic, and that travelers in their land sometimes were badly used.

At length he crossed a high, rugged mountain range and skied out onto a broad plain, mostly treeless, that he had been told marked the beginning of the land of the Magyars. The mountains

had shielded it from the worst of the storm, and
men were able to move about on horseback through
the four decimeters of wind-packed snow. As he
was crossing a frozen river, he saw several mounted
men riding along the high bank opposite him.
They stopped to watch, and as he drew nearer,
he saw that they carried lances. Suddenly one of
them urged his horse down the bank and the others followed, charging toward Nils. The windpack
allowed them to run their horses at a full gallop
on the ice, and the leader dipped his lance as if to
skewer the trespasser. Nils stood calmly without
unslinging his bow or drawing his sword. At the
last moment the rider swerved past him, his horse's
hooves throwing snow on Nils, his left knee almost
touching him. The others drew up in front of the
northman while the leader pulled his mount around
tightly and circled, looking down at him with eyes
squinted against the snow glare. He spoke in a
language unlike any Nils had heard and which he
assumed was Magyar. Getting no answer, the man
spoke again in what Nils recognized as German. In
Anglic Nils said, "I am a mercenary who has come
to seek service with King Janos of the Magyars."

The horsemen looked at one another, talking in
Magyar. Nils sensed that none had understood him.
Speaking slowly and deliberately he said, "Janos.
King Janos. I come to serve Janos."

The leader scowled grotesquely at that, and Nils
sensed his irritation. He spoke rapidly to his men,
and one of them reached down to prod the northman
with his lance and then to gesture toward the
bank they had come from. They made way for him
and he started toward it, two falling in behind
while the others trotted their horses toward the

point at which he had first seen them and disappeared.

They marched him for an hour and a half before he saw the large castle on the open rolling plain. He was taken to the guard room, where a man who was clearly an officer looked up at him and spoke with his captors in Magyar. Then, in good Anglic, he asked, "Where are you from?"

"From Svealann."

The officer snorted. "I have never heard of it," he said, as if that disposed of Svealann. "What have you come here for?"

"I heard of a king called Janos, and I have come to seek service with him."

Even as he finished the statement, Nils sensed that he was in trouble. "Janos, eh? This is the land of Lord Lajos Nagy, and there is no love here for the tyrant Janos." With that he snapped a sharp command in Magyar and one of Nils's captors pressed a sword tip to his back while a guard came forward with manacles.

The dungeon was simply a long spiral staircase that wound its way down underground. Instead of cells it had small open alcoves where prisoners could be chained to the wall by an ankle and wrist. They passed no prisoners as they went down, but from where he was chained Nils could easily sense others below. The only light came from smoky oil lamps, one of which was bracketed to the stone wall opposite each alcove.

The guard who brought him his evening gruel carried a cat-o'-nine-tails in one hand, its leather thong looped about his wrist. Carefully he sized up the new prisoner and took pains to come no nearer than necessary, putting the bowl down where Nils had to stretch for it. As soon as he had it in his hand, Nils threw the hot gruel at him. Reflexively the guard lashed at him, cursing loudly. Nils grabbed the whirring knout and jerked, the loop around the guard's wrist pulling him within reach of Nils's chained hand. Strongly though briefly the guard struggled, but did not cry out.

He had no key. Still chained, Nils took his cap, harness, short sword and cloak, tore strips from the bottom of the cloak and tied the corpse's arms and doubled legs against his torso. Then, one-handed, he threw the corpse down the steep stairs as hard as he could, listening with satisfaction to its rolling, bouncing descent. Next he put the cap on his head, draped the cloak over his shoulders, and squatted, waiting.

After some time the screech of hinges sounded faintly down the stone stairwell, and a voice called down questioningly. Nils huddled against the wall as if in pain—knees, one elbow and head on the stone floor, the short sword in his free hand concealed by the cloak—trying to look like a sick or injured guard in the semi-darkness, watching through slitted eyes. Within a few moments two guards appeared around a turn just above him, the first carrying a torch in one hand, both with short swords drawn. They were scanning the stairs ahead of them and might have passed entirely without seeing him.

Nils groaned softly as the second guard was passing the alcove. The man stopped and stared at him, then stepped in, bending and blocking the light. Quickly Nils raised his body, grabbing the guard's cloak with his chained hand and plunging the short sword into his abdomen and chest. For a

moment he held the sagging form upright, letting
go his sword to do it. The other guard sensed that
something was wrong and moved into the alcove
to see. Nils let the body collapse, reached out from
beneath it with his manacled hand to grab an
ankle, and groped for his short sword again. The
struggling guard began to yell. Nils partly heaved
the corpse from his back and, still clinging to the
kicking ankle with an iron grip, hamstrung the
man, pulled his falling body in close and began to
chop at his back. The guard screamed twice before
the blade split his rib cage.

Nils found a key and unlocked his manacles,
listening intently both with ears and psi sense.
The only pickup was a frozen intentness from
farther down in the dungeon, where he had sensed
other prisoners earlier. If the yells had penetrated the door above, anyone who'd heard them
must have interpreted them as normal dungeon
sounds.

Nils moved quietly down the stairs carrying
the dropped torch and with two harnesses and
swords over one shoulder and one at the waist.
The first prisoner he found stared at him through
hard eyes. The man had the build of a fighter, a
knight, and looked as if he'd been there for a few
days at most.

"Do you want one of these?" Nils asked, touching a scabbard.

The man's mind flashed understanding of his
Anglic. "Let me have it," he answered grimly, and
Nils freed him.

The next prisoner was gaunt and haggard. The
first spoke with him in Magyar and turned to Nils

for the key. "His leg is in bad shape where the iron has rubbed a sore on his ankle, but he can walk."

Farther down they found a third man, who only sat and stared, slack-mouthed, when spoken to. His bony chained arm was rotten to the elbow and he picked at it with filthy fingers. Nils looked into his mind for a moment, then put his sword to the man's chest and thrust.

At the bottom of the staircase they found a chamber with a rack and other instruments, and a stained block, but no door or corridor leaving the place. In one wall was what looked like a large fireplace, though there was no sign that it had been used as such. The first knight went to it.

"A shaft," he said, "for removing bodies secretly. You look able to climb it and there should be a windlass at the top."

Nils ducked into it and stood. Looking up, he could see nothing but blackness. He pressed his back against the front of it and muscled his way up like an alpinist in a chimney, moving as rapidly as possible. It was a long climb—as high as the stair. When he reached the top, he found the darkness barely alleviated by light diffused from somewhere down a corridor. As the knight had predicted, there was a windlass, and Nils lowered the sling. When the rope slackened, he waited until he felt a tug, then began to crank.

It was the injured man he raised. He had begun to lower the sling once more when suddenly there was a shout from far below. "Hurry! They're coming!" He jerked rope from the windlass then, sending the crank spinning, and stepped astride the narrow dimension of the shaft. There was faint shouting and a cry of "Pull!" Hand over hand he drew on the rope with long strokes, disdaining the slow windlass, and in a few moments the knight grasped the edge of the shaft. Together they hauled him out onto the floor, Nils's breath great heaving gasps from the violence of his exertions, and for a moment he failed to read the mixture of pain and rage in the man's mind. One foot and calf had been sliced by a sword, thrust after him as he had started up.

"Where are we, do you know?" Nils asked when he was able.

"I think so. But we can't get away because they know where we are. Even now there must be men hurrying to cut us off. But this time they'll have to kill me. I don't intend to end up like that one down there."

"I'm going back down," said Nils. "I may have a better chance where they don't expect me."

The two Magyars exchanged brief words. "Good luck then," said the one who spoke Anglic. "And I hope you kill many." They shook hands with Nils and limped away down the dark corridor.

Nils slid down the rope into the torture chamber and moved quickly up the stairs past the bodies of the dead prisoner and the three guards. The door at the top was not locked, and he peered out cautiously into the corridor. There was no one in sight. He opened the door no more than necessary, avoiding the abominable screech of hinges, slipped through, and took the direction away from the guard room.

Within a few strides he heard booted feet behind him, not yet in sight, but he did not hurry, depending on the poor disguise of his blood-squattered quard cloak and cap for protection if seen. Within a few meters a curtain hung to the floor on his left and he pushed through it, finding a flight of stairs. He bounded silently up, then stopped at the uncurtained opening at the top. Slippered feet scuffed the corridor he faced, and a female mind mumbled to itself in Magyar. The feet would either pass by the stairs or turn down them. At the same time he heard the voices of men below, stopped just outside the curtain. Nils realized he was holding his breath. A middle-aged woman passed the stairwell entrance without looking in. Waiting a moment to avoid startling her, he stepped into the corridor behind her and moved in the opposite direction. A door opened and closed, and he sensed the dimming of psi pickup from her.

The voices from below were louder now, as if someone was holding the curtain open while talking, and he hurried. This corridor ended at a window, through which he could see the frozen courtyard a dozen meters below. Without hesitation he turned, opened the door to the nearest chamber and walked in.

A tall bald man, wide-shouldered and wearing a long robe, sat before a fire. He turned his weathered, hawklike face to Nils and rose, speaking coldly in Magyar. Nils responded quietly in Anglic.

"I am a foreigner and do not understand Magyar. I had planned to seek service with King Janos but was imprisoned here because this lord has no love for his king. But I killed three guards and escaped, and now they are hunting for me. Call out and you're a dead man."

*   *   *

Nils, his hair cut and wearing the livery of Lord Miklos, sat a horse among Lord Miklos' guard troop. Miklos' voice spoke clearly in the frosty morning air.

"I will repeat the warning, Lajos," he said in Magyar. "You owe your fief to the crown, and homage, and the taxes and services prescribed by law. Twice you've failed those taxes and the respect that should accompany them. The next time Janos will send an army instead of an ambassador. Those were his words. Think about them. And if duty means little to you, consider how precious you hold your life."

With that he turned his horse and, followed by his guard troop, rode stiff-backed across the iron-frozen courtyard and over the bridge.

11.

Lord Miklos looked tired and grim when Nils was ushered into his chamber. The young barbarian didn't need psi to know the reason; Janos II had died unexpectedly during Miklos' absence and Janos III had ascended the throne.

"You traveled far to serve King Janos," Miklos said. "And now he is dead. And while I know little about you, what I do know I like. I will be happy to have you serve me, if you wish to."

"Thank you, my lord," Nils answered. "But I was to serve King Janos, and a Janos sits on the throne. Therefore, I will ask to serve him. If he refuses, and if you still want me, I will be happy to serve you."

Miklos walked to the window and stared out, then turned and spoke carefully in explanation. "Janos III is not the man you sought to serve, nor the same kind of man. If it wasn't for the family resemblance and the nobility of his mother, I could hardly credit the elder with the fathership. Janos II was a noble man, fair, firm, and honorable, a man well fitted to rule. The son, on the other hand, is at best shallow and petty, and it will seldom occur to him that there are considerations beyond his momentary whim. He is devious without the compensation of cleverness, gives no man his confidence and heeds no counsel.

"But the worst that is said of him is only rumor, I hope without grounds—that he will tolerate, if not actually sanction, the vile cult of Baalzebub. Perhaps I shouldn't have told you that, for I've seen nothing that can stand as evidence. But I fear. Not the man, but what he may bring."

"Nonetheless," Nils replied, "I must seek service with King Janos. It was forseen by a seeress whose worth I value highly."

"You believe in seers?"

"I believe in this seeress, for I know her powers. They saved my life once."

"And so she commands you."

"No. But what she said seemed right to me."

"I see. Well, I will not recommend you to the new king. Any recommendation from me he'd take as grounds for suspicion." Miklos looked long and perplexedly at Nils, then rose and held out his hand. "But I give you my best wishes. If you are refused, or enter his service and wish to withdraw, let me know."

The sergeant was explaining to the guard master. "He said he'd come several hundred kilometers to seek service with King Janos. He doesn't even speak Magyar and I had to use Anglic with him. But he's a giant"—the sergeant motioned with his hand somewhat above the height of his own helmet—"and something about him gives me the feeling that he's a real fighter and not just an oaf. And you know how his Majesty likes size in his personal guards."

"All right, Bela, I'll look at him. His Highness is tolerant of foreigners. But he'll have to look very good before I'll ask the men to put up with some-one who speaks no Magyar."

The big iron stove was hot, and Nils, after the manner of the neovikings, had hung both jacket and shirt on a peg. Disdaining a bench, he squat-ted with his back to the wall, paring his nails with a large belt knife. When the two knights entered the guard room he arose, calmly and with a smooth-ness of movement that made the guard master suspect he might do, at that. After a few questions he sent a guardsman to Janos, asking for an audience. Shrewdly, he had Nils leave his jacket and shirt on the peg and took him to Janos with his torso bare except for harness.

Janos was a man of ordinary size, his face domi-nated by the pointed nose and red mustache of his father's line. Nils sensed no evil in him, nor any-thing else remarkable, only a mediocrity of energy and smallness of vision. At the king's command Nils rose from his knees. Janos' blue eyes examined him minutely without his face betraying his judg-ment, but Nils sensed that this was a man who was readily impressed by physical strength.

"Where are you from?" the king asked at length.

"From Svealann, Your Majesty."

"Svealann. And where might that be?"

"Far to the north, Your Majesty. Beyond the lands of the Germans lies the northern sea. Across the sea the Jötar dwell, and north of them the Svear. Beyond the Svear, no one lives."

"Ah. And is it true that in the north, so far from the sun, the lands are colder and snowier?"

"Yes, Your Majesty."

"Then Svealann must be a terrible land. I don't blame you for leaving it. But why did you come all this way to seek service with the king of the Magyars, when there are other kings and realms, some closer?"

"A seeress told me that I would, Your Majesty, and so I did."

"A seeress!" Nils sensed that this impressed the king strongly. "And what seeress was that?"

"A woman who lives in the forest, Your Majesty, and talks to the wolves. Her name is Ilse."

Janos examined this indigestible bit and dropped it. "And do you fight well?"

"I'm told that I fight very well, Your Majesty."

Janos turned to the guard master. "Ferenc, let me see him tested."

For an instant the guard master was dismayed. Somehow he'd neglected to test the man! Suppose he was an oaf after all! "I will test him myself, if that will be all right, Your Highness."

"Fine. That will be abundantly demanding."

The guard master spoke to one of the throne guards, who went to Nils and handed him a sword and shield. Nils handled the sword lightly, its weight and balance registering on his neuro-muscular system. Then they faced each other with swords at the ready. The guard master began the sword play slowly, examining Nils's moves. Nils was content to parry and counter. The guard master's speed increased, and Nils sensed his growing approval. A sudden vigorous and sustained attack failed to make an opening, and the guard master stepped back, sweating in the heated throne room.

"He is very good, Your Highness," he said, turning to the king. "He's surprisingly quick and knows all the moves. His teacher must have known his business. If we'd been fighting instead of sparring, I would have been hard pressed, for then his great strength would have begun to count."

Later, in his chamber, the king ran for his privy counselor, a man whose role no others in the palace knew. And if any suspected, they kept careful silence. The man came at the king's call.

"Did you read the man that Ferenc brought to me for the guard?" Janos asked.

"Yes."

"What did you see in him? And was he telling the truth about a seeress?"

"He was truthful at all times, m'lord. I was limited in reading him because his native tongue is unfamiliar to me, but I assure you he was truthful. I believe he is unable to lie."

"You're joking!"

The counselor bowed slightly. "I never joke, Your Highness. There is that about him which makes me believe he is unable to lie."

"Amazing. That must truly be a handicap."

Sometimes you are almost discerning, the counselor thought to himself. And ordinarily I would agree with that reaction. I wish the swine held discourse with himself. I've never known anyone before who could stand fully conscious for several minutes and not talk to himself within his mind. And it isn't a screen. I will watch him carefully.

*   *   *

The guard soon accepted Nils as one of them, despite their normal animosity toward foreigners. In sparring he was never bested, but even so, the men sensed that he held himself in, and they interpreted that correctly as a desire to avoid making anyone look bad. His disposition was mild and harmonious. And he learned quickly, so that in a few weeks he could converse slowly on a fair assortment of subjects.

One day of his first week Nils was being instructed in Magyar by Sergeant Bela, when a boy in his early teens entered the guard room; he was dressed as a squire and spoke to the sergeant. Bela turned back to Nils.

"This is Imre Rakosi, Nils, a squire to the king. He wants to talk to you through me, as he doesn't have much confidence in the little Anglic he speaks. First he wants to know if it's true that you are a great swordsman."

"It is true," Nils said. He sensed an openness and honesty in the boy.

"And is it true that you come from a barbaric land far from the sun and have traveled in many lands?"

"That's true, too," Nils admitted. "Except that I have traveled only in several lands."

Bela repeated in Magyar, then turned back to Nils. "Imre would like to become fluent in Anglic. And he believes it would be better to learn it from you than from some other tutor. You cannot lapse into Magyar, and in the learning he hopes to hear about lands and customs that we know little of in our land. Will you teach him?"

"I'll be glad to."

The boy addressed Nils directly now, in Anglic.

"Thank you," he said carefully, holding out his hand. Nils shook it.

"He would like to begin after supper this evening," Bela said, "in the outer hall, for it's always open and the benches there are comfortable. If he can't be there, he'll get word to you. Is that all right?"

"Certainly," said Nils, and Imre Rakosi left.

"Are squires here the sons of knights only?" Nils asked.

"Usually. This one is the son of Lord Istvan Rakosi of the eastern marches."

"And was he sponsored earlier by the older king, Janos II?"

"No, he's been with Janos III for almost eight years, since the boy was seven and old enough to serve as a page. The king is a widower, and childless," the sergeant went on. "This boy is like a son to him. And he's a good lad, as Janos is a good master."

Nils had the third and fourth watches—from 0800 to 1600—and his duties were primarily two. When Janos held court, Nils was one of his personal guards, standing behind his throne to its right. At other hours, when Janos was in the throne room, Nils's post was outside the thick door.

And in a chamber behind the throne room, a lean, dark-brown man sat in a black robe reading the mind of the king's visitors. But always, whether Nils stood by the throne or outside the heavy door, the secret counselor monitored the big warrior's mind with one small part of his superbly sensitive psychic awareness. He received almost nothing in the way of either thoughts or emotions there, however, for mostly Nils simply received, sorting and filing data of almost every kind without discussing it with himself.

But the evidence was increasingly unmistakable.

One winter evening the counselor took from a small chest a gray plastic box, closed a switch, and patiently waited. He didn't wait long. As a hair-like needle twitched on the dial, a voice in his mind commanded him.

His mind reviewed the event of Nils's arrival and what he had observed, the little he had been able to learn from Nils's mind, and what he had learned from the minds of others when they had thought about Nils. "And there is no question," he thought, "the barbarian is a psi, and I feel he is not here accidentally. I don't know any details, for I can read nothing specific myself. But you could force him, Master."

His thoughts paused, as if hesitating, and there was a sharp painful tug at the counselor's mind that made him wince and continue.

"And today, as I watched, I became aware that he knows I am here, and that he let me know purposely, realizing I would know it was on purpose. Of course, he could easily know of me from the king's mind. But he knows more about me than the king does; it may be he knows all that I am.

"And he as an undisturbed as a stone."

That winter at Pest was the coldest of memory, Nils was told. Old people, and even the middle-aged, complained that winters were longer and colder than when they were young. But even recent winters had had frequent days when tempera-

tures rose above freezing, weather when the surface
of the ground thawed to mud. This winter it remained like stone. The snow from the great October storm had never been much deeper at Pest
than a man's knees, and little new snow had been
added. Yet until late March the ground remained
covered, except on strong south slopes and near
the south sides of buildings.

The River Danube, which the Magyars called
Duna, froze deeply, and boys and youths fastened
skates to their feet for sport, while people of every
age cut holes through the ice and fished for pike
and sturgeon. Not until April did the ice soften
enough that several fishermen fell through to be
carried away beneath it by the current.

By that time Nils had taken opportunities to
examine maps, but had made no plans. When the
time came, he would have a plan. Meanwhile, he
worked, ate, slept, and learned, finding life quite
agreeable. Imre Rakosi had learned to speak the
simple Anglic tongue quite creditably, while Nils,
living with the Magyar tongue, had substantially
mastered its agglutinative complexities. The two
youths had become close friends.

At the beginning of April they had the first days
of true spring that promise summer. On one such
day both were free from duty, and they rode together along a muddy, rutted road above the Duna,
watching the fishermen standing in the shallow
water that flowed across the gray and spongy ice.
But on a shirt-sleeve day in April they found little
inspiration in the sight of a river still ice-bound.
So they left the bank and turned their horses up
the rubble-paved road to Old Pest.

Old Pest had been immensely larger than the

present town. Around Old Pest lay the open plain, grazed in summer or planted with wheat. But Old Pest itself was an extensive forest, mainly of oak but with other broad-leaved trees, its openings overgrown with hazel brush. The rubble and broken pavement prevented cultivation, at the same time concentrating rainwater in the breaks so that trees could sprout and grow. Here and there parts of a building still stood above the trees. The rest had fallen to storms and the gradual deterioration of material. Over the centuries many building stones had been hauled away to be used in the growth of New Pest, and concrete had been crushed for remanufacturing. Even steel construction rods had been broken and hauled away, to be stacked in smithies for cleaning and reuse. And the paving stones of New Pest came from the rubble of the Old.

The present town had grown up several kilometers from the edge of the old city. Neither merchants, nobles, nor commoners cared to house near its ancient ghosts, nor to the cover it provided to bandits and other predators.

Imre had never been in Old Pest before. Bears, wolves and wild dogs actually were few there in these times, for herdsmen organized hunts, with hounds and scores of armed and mounted men, to hold down depredations. And bandits usually were only transient there, for soldiers of the king hunted them. But explorers occasionally disappeared and were not seen again or were found dead and sometimes mutilated.

Imre and Nils poked cautiously about in one building whose lower levels still stood, and wondered whether it could ever have housed men.

There were no stoves or fireplaces, or anything to take away smoke, or anything to see except debris. "I like it better outside than in here," Nils commented.

"You're right. Let's go back out. Anyway, there's only one building I really want to see. I've looked at it from a distance through the palace windows and the whole immense thing seems still to be standing. It may be farther than we have time to go, though, and maybe we wouldn't be able to find it in this wilderness anyway."

They mounted and went farther on among the trees. "Do you mean the building with the huge dome?" Nils asked.

"That's the one. It is said to be a church."

"And what is, or was, a church?" Nils wanted to know.

"Well," explained Imre, "in the olden times men believed in imaginary beings who were thought to be very powerful and therefore had to be given gifts and sung to, and in general the people had to debase themselves before them. Even the nobility; even kings. And great palaces called churches were built and dedicated to the chief of those beings, who was called Christianity."

"I'm surprised I never heard of him before," Nils said.

"It is said that belief in him died out before the Great Death. Perhaps in your land even the memory was lost, or perhaps it never existed there."

They were passing the base of a great hill of rubble upon which stood only scattered shrubs and scrubby trees, but numerous stalks of forbs lay broken, suggesting that in season it would be alive with wild flowers. Turning their horses, they rode toward its top, hoping to get a better directional fix from its elevation.

"I've heard," Nils remarked, "that some Magyars now believe in a supernatural being called Baalzebub. Have any churches been built to him?"

"There can't be churches to Baalzebub. It's against the law to follow that cult."

"But wasn't it the elder king who decreed that? There is a rumor that Janos III tolerates it."

"It's a lie," Imre said decisively. "For my lord has told me that the cult of Baalzebub is vile and that if I ever have anything to do with it, I will be exiled." He paused and looked upward. "I guess our sunshine is gone, and this rising wind is cold. Do you want to go on or shall we go back to Pest?"

"Let's go back," Nils answered, and they rode briskly down the slope into the trees.

"Nils, why did you ask about Baalzebub?"

"Not through any wish to offend you, I promise you that."

"I believe you," Imre said. "But let me explain something that may make things clearer to you. There are those who dislike our lord because he is not the strong and open man his father was, and they pass evil rumors about him. But I've known him since I was a little boy, almost as long as I can remember, and he has been a second father to me. I know his faults, but I also know he is a good man."

"Did he take you with him on his trip to the lower Duna?"

"No. He took none of his household except for five guards. I was only ten then. And he went only as far as the Serbland, not the lower Duna."

"Was it from there he brought his dark-skinned counselor?"

"Dark-skinned counselor?"

"The one named Ahmed."

Imre looked strangely at Nils for a moment, before his frown dissolved into a smile. "Oh, I see. Ahmed is not a counselor, Nils; he is only a personal servant."

"Ah. He is so secretive and his appearance so sinister, I thought he might be a servant of Baalzebub, given to the king to influence him without the king knowing it."

Imre laughed. "Civilization must seem strange to someone from the wild north. No, Nils, Ahmed is not secretive, only shy. And as for sinister, others feel the same about that as you do. But it is only his blackness, for which he can thank a scorching eastern sun.

A strong gust of wind rattled the bare branches above them. "Look, snowflakes!" Nils said. In a few moments the air was swirling with them, and Nils and Imre spurred their horses to a trot, where trails permitted, until they came out of the forest. Then, faces glowing from exhilaration and wet snow, they galloped down the road to Pest.

And from that time Nils was prepared for a trip down the Duna, possibly in chains, unless of course, he was murdered. For Ahmed would certainly read Imre, and Kazi would either want to examine this barbarian psi himself or have him dead.

Within weeks the message came to Janos by a courier in livery richer than the people of Pest had even seen, along with a troop of tall, swarthy horsemen on animals that awed even the great

Magyar horse breeders. Kazi sent it this way instead of through Ahmed in order to keep the psi tuner secret from Janos.

"Ahmed," Janos said, "I won't stand for it. Why does he want me to send the boy to him?"

Ahmed looked thoughtfully at the soft bleached parchment as if he hadn't already known what would be written there or why. "Perhaps he doesn't trust you."

"But that's nonsense. Why shouldn't he trust me? I've done nothing to earn his distrust."

"I don't *know* that he distrusts you, but that would explain his request. Remember, you are hundreds of kilometers away from him, and so he has no way of looking into your mind. He is used to knowing the minds of everyone around him, and is impatient when he doesn't."

"So he wants the boy as a hostage, then," Janos snapped. "He can't have him."

"Why not?" Ahmed asked. "You know he'll treat him like a prince, for he depends on you, and youth enjoys the adventure of strange lands. You could send the giant barbarian with him as bodyguard and companion, for they are close friends."

Janos sat quietly for a few minutes, his face still angry at first, then gradually grim, and finally thoughtful. "All right," he said at last. "I'll do it. Imre and the barbarian on my royal barge, and a detail from my guard. I will also provide a barge for the courier troop and they can leave their horses with me as a gift." He looked at Ahmed, thin-lipped. "But I do not like this hostage business, for I gave him my word and I am not used to being treated like this."

12.

While a man was chief of the Svear, his home village would be known as Hövdingeby, the Chief's Village. During the chieftainship of Axel Stornäve, Hövdingeby was in perhaps the greatest farm clearing in Svealann, called Kornmark for the barley that once was grown there. Now barley could not be relied on to mature its grain, and it was rye that filled the bins after harvest.

Kornmark covered a somewhat irregular area of about two by five kilometers, broken here and there by birch groves, swales, and heaps of stones that had been picked from the fields. There were three villages in Kornmark, one near each end and one near the center, each covering a few hectares. Each was a rough broken circle of log buildings— the homes, barns and outbuildings of the farmers— surrounding a common ground. In the middle of the common was the longhouse, which contained a feasting hall, guest lodgings, and the communal steam bath.

It was late May, when the daylight lasts for more than eighteen hours. Normally in that season cattle would have been in the fields, fattening on new grass, and the air would have been pungent with smoke as the boys and women burned off last year's dead grass in the surrounding pasture woods. But this year the fields were still soft brown mud, while along the leeward sides of the stone fences there still lay broad, low drifts of granular snow.

A thin, cold rain drove out of the west against the backs of two warriors who were walking across the clearing on the cart road. Their leather breeches were dark with rain, and the fur of their jackets was wet and draggled. In the forest, where spruce and pine shaded the trails, they had run on skis. Now each carried his skis on one wide shoulder, with his boots slung over the other, and the deep tracks of their tough bare feet filled at once with icy water.

Big flakes of snow began to come with the rain.

Near the east end of the clearing, above the high bank of a river, was Hövdingeby, which also was called Vargby because it was the original home of the Wolf Clan and its major village. The longhouse there measured thirty meters, and many men could sleep in its steep-roofed loft. Its logs had been squared with broad ax and adze so that they fitted almost perfectly, and even the stones of its smoking chimneys had been squared. At each end the ridgepole thrust out three meters beyond the overhanging roof, curving upward, scrolled and bearing the carven likeness of a wolf. Hides covered its windows, scraped thin to pass more light, but on the westward side the shutters were closed against the rain.

The two warriors walked up its split-log steps and scraped their muddy feet on the stoop. One rapped sharply on the plank door with the hilt of his knife, and a stout thrall woman let them in. It was cold and gloomy in the entry room. Though Svear, the two warriors were not of the Wolf Clan, so they waited there with the silence of men who had nothing new to say to each other and were disinclined to talk for the sake of breaking silence. Shortly a tall old man, Axel Stornäve himself, came out to them wearing a loose cloak of white hare skins. "You are the last to arrive," he said. "I'm sorry my messenger took so long to find you." The hands that gripped could have crushed necks.

"We are often gone from our homes," one answered. "Reindeer are not cattle. The herds must range far for forage."

The old man ushered them into the hall. "We have dry clothes for you," he said. "I'll have food warmed, and the stones are hot in the bath house. When you have bathed and eaten, I suggest you rest. We will meet together at the evening meal, and it may be late before the talking ends."

The men at the evening meal were the chiefs of the three tribes, with their counselors, and the clan chieftains of the Svear, each with his lieutenant. They ate roast pig, that most savory of flesh, smoked salmon, and blood pudding thickened with barley and sweetened with honey that had found its way there from southern Jötmark. And there·was fermented milk, and ale, but no brännvin, for these men were sometimes enemies who had put aside their feuds to meet together. Axel Stornäve did not want the blood to run too warm in their veins.

When the platters were taken away, Stornäve

rose, the oldest man of them, and they all listened, for warriors and raid leaders did not live as long as he had without skill and luck and cunning.

"Some in my clan," he said, "and in all the clans of the Svear, have talked in recent years of leaving our land. They have heard of lands where the summers are longer and warmer. And I have heard it is the same among the Jötar and Norskar." He turned toward the bull-like form of Tjur Blodyxa, chief of the Jötar. "I have heard that in Jötmark the Sea Eagle Clan began last summer to build large boats, ships in which to send strong war parties to find a better land. It was also told at the last ting of the Svear"—here he turned grimly to Jäävklo of the Gluttons—"that our own northern clans whisper of breaking the bans and trying to take away land from the clans to the south, unless we willingly make room for them.

"And now we have had this winter unlike any before, and our people wonder if we can make a crop. We have had to kill many cattle, poor in flesh, because the hay barns were becoming empty, and it's better to kill some than lose all. But we have butchered the seed, so calves will be few. And we cannot live on wild flesh, for there are too many of us." He paused and looked around at the faces turned toward him. "So I believe the Sea Eagles have the right idea," he went on. "The time has come to leave.

"But the lands to the south are peopled already. We have all heard wanderers who have been to some of them. A wanderer of your Otter Clan"—he turned again to Tjur Blodyxa—"has told us stories in this very longhouse of the Daneland where he had lived, where the clearings are greater than the forests, and the warriors have high stone walls to protect them. And when I questioned him he said that in the Daneland, too, people complained that the winters were growing longer and harder.

"And from your Seal Clan"—he turned to Isbjørn Hjeltesøn, chief of the Norskar—"a wanderer told us of the Frisland, south across the sea, where the people speak a tongue he could not understand, where there are few trees, and the pastures and haylands are so wide a man can't see across them. There they complain that each year they must build their haystacks bigger and haul more wood from the distant forests.

"Is the whole world freezing? Or are there really lands where the summers are long and warm? We all have heard rumors of them. But how does one come to such lands? There is one man of the Wolf Clan who may be the greatest traveler of all. Last fall he returned from four years of absence, telling tales of the lands he had visited. He is Sten Vannaren; you can talk to him later and ask him questions. He brought with him what you see on this wall." The old chief turned and pulled a bearskin from the pegs on which it had hung, exposing a map of Europe. "This is a map the craft of whose makers far exceeds ours. It is said to be a copy of a map of the ancients and is made on a stuff called linen. North is at the top, as on the maps we make ourselves. Here"—his big finger circled—"are the lands of the tribes. The blue is the sea."

Axel Stornäve looked around the table. All eyes were on the marvel before them, so he continued talking and pointing. "Sten journeyed across several lands and finally came to this southern sea. And he found that what we had believed is actually true: that as you continue southward the sun gets nearer and higher and the climate warmer. The lands around that sea are never cold except high in the mountains, and even in the heart of winter the snows lie on the ground for only a few days at a time, or a few weeks at worst.

"It is a land where the clans could be happy.

"There are two ways to reach that land. One is by sea." He traced a route from the Skagerrak across the North Sea, southward along the Atlantic coast and through Gibraltar. Grim eyes watched. "Although perhaps we would not have to go that far. This might serve as well." He pointed to the coast along the Bay of Biscay. "But if every fishing boat left filled with warriors, they still would be too few. By the time the boats could make a second trip, those few would be dead at the hands of the tribes who live there now.

"The second way is across the land, after boats have made the short trip here." He ran his finger along the shores south of the Baltic. "The tribes of each land we entered would fight, of course, and their people are very numerous, so there are many of them for each one of us. In some of those lands the chiefs hire foreigners in their armies, so Sten never went hungry for food or fight. And their warriors, which they call knights, are less skilled with weapons than we. Also, their warriors do not care to go on foot. If they must go into battle on foot, they prefer to delay. He even found some who would hardly be able to fight after a day's march. Do not be mistaken. They have fierce men, men not afraid to die"—here the old chief paused for effect, then spoke slowly and clearly—"but never did he find any knight who was a match for one of our warriors.

"Even so, if the Sea Eagle Clan landed here"—he pointed to northern Poland—"at the nearest place to their homeland, and started south, the knights of that district would attack them on horse-back and kill many. And the chief of that land would gather a strong army, of many hundreds, and attack until no man of the Sea Eagles was left alive, they would be so outnumbered. And what then of their women and children and the spirits of their dead?

"But here is a place of low sand hills along the coast, covered with forest, and only a few fishermen live there." He pointed to a stretch of Polish coast. "And behind the sand hills are marshes, where knights cannot cross on their horses. If the Sea Eagles landed there, it is likely that they would not be strongly attacked so long as they stayed there.

"And what if the Otter Clan followed, and the Bears, and then others? This district behind the coast," he continued, his big finger circling inland, "also has large forests. If enough warriors landed on the coast, they might march in strength and defend and hold some of the forest while still more of the people landed—freeholders, women, children and thralls. If *all* the clans landed there, I believe they could then cross the lands to the south, regardless of the armies raised against them, and take and hold a land near the southern sea."

The old chief looked around the split log table for a moment without speaking, and a small smile began to play around the corners of his wide mouth. "I see that Jäävklo of the Gluttons wants me to sit

so that he may speak. He wants to ask me how I
propose to move the tribes across the sea in a few
score fishing boats that cannot take more than a
dozen men each, besides the oarsmen.

"I led the Wolf Clan before I was chosen chief of
the Svear, and I have talked about this to the
warrior who now is chieftain of the Wolves, Ulf
Vargson. He in turn held council with his warriors
and freeholders. And it is agreed. The Wolf Clan
will send out half a dozen fishing boats of warriors
with Sten Vannaren to guide them. They will find
this place I spoke of," he pointed, "land the warriors and come back for more.

"But on the second trip, all our boats will go,
and most of them will go here"—he pointed to a
harbor on the Polish coast—"where there are ships
large enough to carry a hundred men besides the
oarsmen. And they will seize such of those ships as
they can, returning here with them."

Strong yellow teeth began to show in the torch-
light around the table.

"The Wolf Clan would go alone if they had to,
but I know they won't have to. I know the other
clans too well, from many raids and fights. And
the Sea Eagles had decided to go before we did. If
all the clans unite, our combined strength can
bring us to the southern sea.

"Look!" Axel Stornäve knelt for a moment and
picked up a bundle of pine branches that had lain
on the floor behind his seat. He held one branch
up and snapped it in his hands. "By itself it has
little strength," he said. "But now"—he took as
many together as he could wrap his huge hands
around, with a great effort strove to break them,
then held them overhead unbroken.

"Which of you will go back to your people and join them with us?"

Every man around the table stood, most of them shouting approval. Axel still stood, with one hand in the air, and in a few moments the others settled to the benches again, aware that he was not done.

"I knew it," he said. "And when you take this matter to your people, they will agree to it, for this winter has caused every man to think. But we can't delay. If we can make no crop this summer except of hay, and if next winter is at all like this one has been, we will be weak and hungry in another year. We must all be gone before winter comes again. Nor can we winter across the sea except in force, for we must be able to take what we need by force from the people there.

"Our harbor is free of ice now, at last. Our people already have been killing the rest of the cattle and drying the meat over fires. We will send the first boats on the day after tomorrow, the weather willing. After our first war parties have landed, two boats will go here." He pointed to the island of Bornholm, between the Swedish and Polish coasts. "One will wait to guide the first boats of the Jötar to the landing place." He looked down the table at one old enemy, Tjur Blodyxa, and then in the other direction at another, Isbjørn Hjeltesøn. "The other will guide the first boats of the Norskar." The old man grinned. "Maybe you can get the Danes to 'loan' you some ships."

A scowl had begun to grow on Tjur Blodyxa's surly face, and he stood without leave. "And who will lead this expedition?" he asked.

Axel Stornäve said nothing for a moment, savoring the surprise he had for the Jöta chief. "Not me," he said. "I'm too old. That leadership is what we must decide next."

It was past midnight. They had agreed that the tribes would act independently in moving their own people, except that the Wolf Clan of the Svear would pick the place. But the war leader of those who had landed would also be of the Svear. Then the clan chieftains of the Svear elected Björn Ärrbuk as war leader. He was the tribe's most famous fighter and its most famous living raid leader. Afterward, they questioned Sten Vannaren about the place they would land and the country where they hoped to go.

Now they were going to bed. Axel Stornäve stepped out the door to look at the night and found new snow ankle-deep on the ground.

13.

KAZI, TIMUR KARIM (A.D. 2064-2831), psionicist and emperor. Born in Kabul, Afghanistan, he received a Ph.D. in neurophysiology from the University of Lucerne in 2087; lectured at London University, 2087-2090; was professor of psionics at Damascus University, 2090-2094; and held the Freimann Chair of Psionics Research at the University of Tel Aviv, 2094-2105.

In 2096, Kazi developed the "esper crystal," which became the functional element of the psi tuner. At age forty-one, although in chronically poor health, he was one of the few survivors of the Great Death of 2105. He also survived the difficult and primitive conditions that followed the plague, presumably by dominating other survivors.

Seriously afflicted with asthma and without effective medicines, he eventually developed a process of ego-transfer believed to involve the use of drugs and the psi tuner, transferring his ego from his aging and debilitated body to one younger and healthier.

As a child, Kazi had been offensively egotistical,

effectively alienating himself from normal human relationships. This trait intensified with his brilliant scientific successes and his increasing ability to read minds and dominate others. His development and use of ego-transfer, with the near immortality it provided, probably furthered the pathological deterioration of his personality.

Sometime about the middle of the twenty-second century, Kazi disappeared. He seems to have developed a self-controlled psionic means of suspended animation. It has been suggested that he used this to mark time until an increased population and further socio-economic development provided something more gratifying to dominate. Legends indicate that he was worshipped as a god at the time he disappeared and that periodic living sacrifices of young men were made at his tomb, believed to have been a cave in the Judean Hills. Perhaps they were used for ego-transfers. If so, he may occasionally have emerged to maintain the legend and select his next body.

He became active again sometime about 2750, and from that time our picture becomes less conjectural again. Gradually he came to dominate the Middle and Near East as far south as the Sudan, as well as much of the Balkans, ruling some of the territory directly and some of it as tributary provinces.

Kazi developed a culture specifically for his army. Each level practiced a harsh domination of the lower ranks, and all ranks brutalized slaves and subject peoples. The utmost in cruelty was not merely permitted, but demanded of the soldiers. Discipline was based on fear, the fellowship of mutual depravity, and a supersititous awe and terror of the ruler. He called them "orcs," after an army of subhuman monsters in a classic of pre-plague fantasy fiction, The *Lord of the Rings*. (*See* Tolkien, J.R.R.) After the first or second generation, all orcs resulted from forced matings between his soldiers and captive women, the offspring growing up in vicious camps whose regimens were designed to eliminate the weak and to produce the orc personality.

This was Earth's largest post-plague army, and its only standing army. Its men were better disciplined and trained than their feudal contemporaries and could be relied upon to fight viciously and skillfully. It was also versatile, serving as both infantry and cavalry during a time when feudal armies and most barbaric tribes despised foot warfare.

Kazi himself built in its major weakness when he designed its culture. Its primary orientation was not fighting, but occupying and brutalizing. It was supreme in breaking conquered peoples and served its master's psycopathic compulsion for unbridled depravity, but it lacked the fervor and vigor necessary for a really great army in an age of edged weapons and close combat.

Kazi relied on auxiliaries to supplement that shortcoming. Many small tribes of "horse barbarians" ranged and fought one another in the steppes and arid mountains of south-central Asia as far west as Turkey. By combinations of privilege, flattery and threats, he was able to unite and command the use of large numbers of those tribesmen when he wished, mostly to control other similar tribes. The horse barbarians sometimes lacked discipline and unit coordination, but they were skilled and reckless cavalry whose passion was fighting. . . .

(From *The New School Encyclopedia*, copyrighted A.C. 920, Deep Harbor, New Home.)

14.

The Duna had carried them out of the Hungarian prairie through forested mountains, and then eastward for several days through open grasslands again, with hills to the south and broad plains and marshes to the north. Occasionally they passed herds of cattle accompanied by mounted horsemen, and when they were near enough, Nils could see that they carried no weapons, except short bows to protect their herds from wolves. He realized they must have entered Kazi's realm.

Nils and Imre had carefully studied the map that Janos had given Imre. Therefore, they were expecting it when the river turned north and the barges left it to enter a great canal, built by the ancients, that left the Duna and struck eastward like an arrow toward the sea. On its north bank would stand the City of Kazi.

After a number of kilometers, an obsidian tower could be seen glistening blackly at a distance, and as the current carried them rapidly along, they soon saw other buildings of dark basalt. They were passing kilometers of barbarian camps on the north side of the canal, with the banners of many tribes moving in the wind above the tents. Men in mail or leather shirts, or their own leathery skins, rode at sport or in idleness, sometimes stopping to watch intently the richly ornamented barges.

In a sense the City of Kazi was a military camp, for its purpose was to house his orcs. But it was much more than a camp, for no town could match its engineering and order. From the palace with its tower, rows of dark stone buildings radiated outward like the spokes of a half-wheel.

The steersmen now were running close to the north bank, and they passed stone granaries and warehouses where stone steps led up from the wharves. Ahead was a balustraded wharf of dark and beautifully figured gneiss, with broad stairs of the same rock climbing to a gardened courtyard in front of the palace. Their steersman shouted, and for almost the first time the oars were wetted, backing water briefly to slow the barge almost to a halt as they approached the wharf. Naked brown men, some nearly black, handled the line, while others, wearing harness and weapons, waited for the passengers. A gangplank of dark burnished wood was laid across the gunwales, and Imre and Nils landed. A fat toga-clad man with a sharp beak of a nose bowed slightly to Imre. In almost falsetto Anglic he announced, "His Holiness has instructed that I escort you to your apartment. Baths and fresh clothing await you there. When you are refreshed, His Holiness would like an audience with you, and I will return to conduct you to him."

"And may my friend accompany me to that audience?" Imre asked.

"His Holiness has specified that both guests should attend, unless"—the steward bowed slightly again—"your Lordship wishes otherwise."

He led them across the courtyard to the palace and up exterior steps to a terrace garden, where, looking eastward into the distance, they caught sight of the sea and a harbor with many ships. Inside, the walls of their apartment were veneered with white marble and hung with soft lustrous blue material. The glazed windows were open and the heavy curtains drawn back so that the rooms were light and airy.

The steward dipped his head again and left.

The white stone baths were as long as Nils's reach and set below the floor. Steps entered them. Imre knelt, dipped his fingers into one, and his breath hissed between his teeth. "My blood!" he gasped. "Are we supposed to bathe or be boiled?"

Nils grinned like a wolf and began to strip. "In my homeland we take steam baths and then roll naked in the snow."

"Huh! I'm glad we're here instead of there then. What do you call it again? I'll be careful never to go there."

"It's called Svealann, and the real reason I was exiled is that they don't tolerate midgets. My growth was stunted from missing too many steam baths." Very carefully he moved down the steps into the water. "I've never confessed it to anyone since I left there," he added, "because it's embarrassing to a northman to be a midget, and I've been keeping it a secret. I hope you won't tell anyone."

Imre had scarcely settled on the sitting ledge in his bath when a dark girl entered the room. Without speaking she set a dish of soap on the low curb beside each bath and left.

"Well!" Imre stared after her indignantly. "They certainly have strange customs here, where women come into a man's bath—and a young, pretty one at that. Say, look, the soap is white! It is soap, isn't it? And smell it. Like a woman's scent. Can stuff like that possibly get us clean?"

Nils stood and began to lather his torso, the sinews in his arms, shoulders and chest flexing and bunching as he washed. Imre stared. "You know," he said, "I'd take steam baths, too, and roll in the snow, if I thought it would grow me muscles like yours."

Nils grinned again, squatted to the neck, lathered his pale hair, and submerged. When he came up, Imre was staring past him in distress. Two young women had entered and stood quietly, holding long fluffy towels. Nils emerged calmly and stood while one of them dried him. Then she left, again without a word. On each of two benches lay clean white clothing, neatly folded. Nils walked to one of them and dressed in loose white pantaloons and a white robe that came to his knees. There was no belt or other ready means for fastening on as much as a dagger.

Imre's expression was pure consternation. "Go!" he said to the remaining girl. "I will dry myself." She turned. "No. Wait." He looked grimly at Nils and climbed quickly from the bath to be dried. He did not speak until he had dressed himself.

"I've never heard of such shameless customs before," he said tightly. "And I'm going to demand that they keep those women out of here before we become degenerate and useless. I . . ."

The soft-faced steward had quietly entered the room and made his slight obeisance. "Your Lordship, the chief of your guard, who calls himself Sergeant Bela, awaits your pleasure."

"Awaits our pleasure!" Imre exploded. "That's more than you know enough to do. Haven't you ever heard of announcing yourself before entering? After this, knock or use a bell or something."

The steward bowed more deeply.

"Now you can tell Bela I'll be happy to see him, and then have some food and drink sent up."

With another bow the steward left, and a moment later they heard firmer footfalls. There was a sharp rapping, as of a dagger haft on the wall beside the door.

"Bela?"

"That's right, m'Lord."

"Come in then. I thought it was you. None of these people around here have the manners to knock."

Bela glanced around the apartment and his lips pursed in a silent whistle. "M'Lord, we're to leave at once, and I wanted to see you before we went. His Highness will ask me if you were properly received, and I wanted to see for myself."

"Why do you have to leave so soon?" Imre asked.

"They've fed us and have horses saddled and waiting—beautiful horses, too, they are. People who breed horseflesh like that can't be all bad. Anyway, they say there aren't enough of us to ride back safely after we leave their borders, because of bandits and other swine. But they have a small caravan bound for somewhere near home, and they've held it for us. They want it to leave right away."

"Well, I guess that's reason enough," Imre said reluctantly. "But I'll miss hearing my own language and seeing good, honest Magyar people. Compared to these people, Nils will seem like a native Magyar. And unless I talk to myself, his is likely to be the only Magyar speech I'll hear." He grinned. "If the next time you see me I speak our language with a sing-song, blame it on our little friend. Meanwhile, tell His Highness that we've been hospitably received and beautifully housed, and I expect that when they've adjusted to our differences in custom, we'll be quite happy."

They walked out together and Bela shook their hands and left.

When Imre and Nils had finished a light meal of sweetened fruit and cream, the steward returned, announcing himself this time with a small bell. Not only his black eyes and bland face were unreadable; the man covered his mind with a wash of no-thought. The household staff here might need to develop that for survival, Nils realized.

"If your Lordship is ready," the steward said, bowing again to Imre, "His Holiness will see you now."

The throne room was in the tower, and even its inner walls were obsidian, but it was well lighted by large windows. The ceiling was no more than four meters high, and its length and width about six meters, to enhance the size of its master. The throne was upholstered and the floor carpeted with rich furs. There were four men there. One was a chamberlain—a thin, pale, expressionless man wearing a toga. Two were tall muscular black men wearing loincloths and holding broad curved swords; one stood on each side of the throne room.

The fourth man was Kazi.

The steward dropped to his knees outside the door and crawled two meters inside, moving his forehead along the floor. Nils had never read such genuine unalloyed fear before. "They are here, Your Highness," he announced in his falsetto, and then crawled out backward, his eyes still directed at the floor.

Outside the door, Imre looked nervously at Nils, uncertain what to do next. Nils stepped forward, entered upright, and bowed, then stood aside as if ushering Imre in. Imre braced himself, set his face, and followed.

Kazi arose. He was easily the largest man either of them had ever seen, something more than two meters tall, and utterly naked. He was neatly jointed but hugely muscled, and grossly, almost unfeasibly, male. His skin was dark—not brown but almost gun-metal blue, like some of the natives of southern India. The lean, aquiline face was a caricature of evil, and a slight, mocking smile showed perfectly white teeth. He appeared to be about thirty years old.

The air was heavy with the power he exuded.

He gestured toward two low cushions on opposite sides of the chamber, each in front of a guard, and remained standing until his visitors were seated. Then he lowered himself to the throne and rested his eyes on Nils.

"I have awaited you with interest."

The Anglic words came from the lips of the chamberlain, but the chamberlain's mind was completely blank, and there was no doubt that the words were from the mind of Kazi.

Nils nodded.

"And you planned that I should have you brought here. Did it occur to you that that would be very dangerous?"

Not a muscle moved in Nils's relaxed face.

"Unless, of course, you came here to take service with me?" Ahmed was right, Kazi thought. He does not screen; his consciousness simply does not talk to itself. I have never seen this before, except in idiots.

"You wouldn't have me in your service," Nils answered calmly.

"Why not?"

"Because you can't read my mind."

Kazi's flash of anger staggered his chamberlain, and even Imre, sitting ignored and bewildered, felt it strongly, blanching. Now Kazi's own lips spoke. "I can read your mind to the finest detail if I wish, if you should survive long enough."

"You're not likely to do that," Nils replied matter-of-factly. "You brought me here because you're extremely curious about me, and there is little in the world that is interesting to you anymore. And you are very old and do not age; time is not important to you. You will wait and explore me with your wits and questions rather than destroy me."

Kazi allowed his brows to raise for a moment, then turned to Imre. "Your large friend thinks I am very old. How old do you take me for?"

Imre was almost afraid to speak. "Thirty?" he replied hesitantly.

"The boy says thirty," Kazi looked at Nils with something like amusement. "Then why do you say I am very old?"

"I sense it."

"You can't see into my mind."

"No, I simply sense it. And if you are very old but look thirty, then it follows that you do not age."

Kazi gazed intently at Nils. "I could have you killed in an instant."

"I have died before."

Kazi's eyes narrowed. "I have heard of that belief. But if it is true, yet you do not remember from one life to the next, what use is it? Meanwhile, you are young and gifted with a great pulsing body that has much yet to enjoy. You do not know how much." Kazi paused, intent for some mental response that did not come, then went on. "And your mind may be one of the two most unusual minds that exist. It would be enormously interesting to see what could be made of it. You can be a ruler in this world if you wish, have and do almost anything you want."

"I have looked at the great glaciers in the valleys of the north," Nils replied. "It is said they are growing toward the sea and that they have grown before and covered the whole land with ice and then disappeared, time and again. Even you won't live until they melt one time, because you couldn't stand it that long. I have looked at the stars on a clear night. They are said to be so far away that from some of them the light I saw has been a thousand times a thousand years coming. So what is this you offer?"

Kazi stared at him for long seconds, then his mind shot out a command. One tall guard raised his sword and swung with all the strength of his powerful right arm and shoulder. Nils was lunging from his seat on the cushion, but the weapon moved too quickly. Imre's head struck the floor without rolling, the carpeting was so thick and soft. Nils felt sharp steel against his back and stared as Imre's body toppled slowly sideways, blood spurting from the neck.

"So. You are subject to emotion, after all," Kazi said pleasantly. "The difference is that there is no positive feedback. It flashed and died. Have you ever thought of yourself as . . ." He paused. There was no word for it which would have meaning for a barbarian, or for any man of this age. "As a computer?" he finished.

Nils sat, relaxed again, watching Kazi without answering.

"And where did you learn about ice ages and the distances between stars?"

"From a wise man."

"Of your own people?"

"No. My people have lost such knowledge. I learned it after I began my travels."

"And why do you believe such strange stories?"

"Because they are true."

"And you sense truth?" Kazi gazed thoughtfully at him for a long minute. "I will think about you for a while. Return to your apartment. And if you want anything—drinks, girls, someone to answer questions—strike the gong you find there. Tomorrow you will attend the games with me. You will find them interesting."

Imre's things still lay on a bench when Nils entered. He struck the gong softly, and very soon a girl appeared to stand silently. "Take these things away," he said. "Their owner is dead."

Apparently the girl understood Anglic because she bent and picked them up.

"Also," Nils added, "I would like the company of someone who can answer my questions."

"I will tell the steward," she said, her voice quiet and accented.

Nils went into his own chamber then. Its window faced west, and the evening sun shone in. He became aware of a sense of depression, and looked at it for a few seconds so that it went away. Drawing the heavy curtains he lay down and closed his eyes, seeming to fall asleep at once. But a part of him remained aware, and after a time he knew that someone was coming up the stairs to the terrace outside. It was a young woman, a psi, and she was coming to find him.

He swung his powerful legs over the side of the bed, got up and walked to the door. The sun had just set, but the western sky was so cloudless and free of haze that it showed little color other than silver blue. The girl was just outside, and stopped, facing him as his big torso blocked the way.

"You were resting; perhaps I came too soon." She phrased her thoughts in Anglic, not speaking. "I am Nephthys. My father directed me to come to you and answer your questions if I am able."

She was awesomely beautiful.

His answer was also unvoiced. "I was waiting, not resting." He stepped back into the room.

She followed, and sat gracefully on a couch. Nils had hardly needed the brief mental identification of "father" she had given him. Her color, psi, and fine-boned face indicated that she was Kazi's daughter.

Nephthys could not read Nils's interpretation, but her knowingness anticipated it. "In a sense he is not my father," her thoughts continued. "The body he wears now is that of a half-brother. But at one time he wore the body of my father—his is the mind, the ego-essence, the continuity of experience, memory and identity, that was, is, my father. It is as father that I think of him. Do you understand?"

"I'm beginning to. He does age, then, but before he becomes old, he somehow occupies a new body without . . . without dying, without forgetting. And he fathers a series of bodies to equip himself properly, the way the lords of the Danes and the Magyars breed special lines of horses in order to have good mounts."

She nodded. "He has two harems, small but highly select. One is of beauties, for pleasure; my mother was one of these. The other is to provide young men from which he can select a physical successor."

"And does he change bodies for special purposes, as a knight may use one horse to travel on, another for hunting and a third for battle?"

"No," she answered, half-smiling at the analogy. "The transfer is difficult, requiring days of preparation, and the drugs for both bodies are unpleasant. His emotions at such a time, and those of the other, are of men fighting with death."

Nils moved to another subject. "And I suppose he plans to march north with his armies very soon."

"How did you know?"

"He concentrated this army of horse barbarians for a reason. And he won't keep them here long because of the problems of feeding them and keeping them from fighting each other out of idleness and boredom. And he already rules these plains and all the lands to the south, while in the west the mountain tribes of the South Slavs give him tribute and slaves. And up the Duna are the Magyars, whose king has agreed to strike north and west with his army at your father's command, into the lands of the Germans and Bohemians. I learned that from the mind of the Magyar king himself. But north of here are the lands of the Ukrainians and Poles, still independent, with rich pastures and farms and large herds of cattle and horses. And a good route to western Europe; there aren't any mountains to cross. But I have only a vague idea of how many men Kazi has."

"I've heard him say he has ten thousand orcs ready to march. That doesn't include garrisons that must be left behind to control the empire. And those ten thousand are equal to twice that number of any other soldiers, in fighting effectiveness. Beyond that he has gathered twenty thousand horse barbarians. Their loyalties are to their chiefs, but he has made those chieftains his."

She stopped then, looking at and into Nils. "This place is deadly for you," she said. "Why did you come here?"

He looked intently back at her, and even her dark skin flushed, because his thoughts were clearly on her and she could not read them.

"Let me ask instead why you came here," Nils countered. "Why did your father send you instead of one of his officers who could answer questions that you can't."

"You know already."

"Only by inference, and not deeply."

"His girl children, if they are beautiful enough, he trains as prizes or gifts or bribes for chiefs and kings. And when they have accepted one of us, they are caught. For there are no others like us, and we are psis. We are trained not only to please them but to influence and control them. But although you are a man, you are a different sort of man, and not predictable. The reason I was chosen instead of another is that I am receptive at this time. Father believes he may have to kill you and that it would be a shame if you died without issue, your genes lost." She looked at Nils without embarrassment. "But as you can see, the thought is not unpleasant to me. I have never known any- one like you. You intrigue me. And my father is right; if you must die, your genes should not be lost."

Nils's mind spoke again to the girl, but his thoughts were framed primarily for her father, whom he knew must be monitoring them. "Kazi senses an attribute in me that he doesn't understand, and he wants it. If not from me, then from my offspring. Despite his own experience he thinks it is heritable. And I'd give it to him if I could, for it would change him." Nils sat with his mind still for a few moments, then thought again. "Your father has more on earth than any other man, but he finds little pleasure in it. And although he may conquer Europe, he won't rule it long, because he is getting ready to die."

In his chamber, Kazi stared unseeingly out at Mars, the evening star, above the horizon. The thoughts he had just overhead were clear enough in his mind, but it refused to analyze them.

15.

In the early morning sunlight the steward discreetly rang his little bell on the terrace, but Nephthys had already left. Nils looked out the door instead of calling him in. "What do you want?" Nils asked.

"I have been sent to waken you so that you may eat before you go to meet His Holiness."

Nils grinned at him. "I'm awake. Where is the food?"

Calmly, without speaking, the steward turned and left. This morning Nils's bath was cool instead of hot. When he had dressed, the quiet girl who had served him the day before brought a tray of soft-boiled eggs, sweetened porridge, berries and milk. He had hardly finished when he heard the steward's little bell again.

As they walked along the terrace and down the stairs, Nils looked out across the city. There were many orcs on foot in the street, while among the distant tent camps outside the city rose the dust clouds of thousands of mounted men. Movement was in the direction of a large stone structure, of a

type unfamiliar to Nils, in an open space at the
end of the city's widest street.

Just outside the courtyard a large bronze char-
iot waited, ornamented with gold and harnessed
to four magnificent black horses. In front and behind were elite guards on comparable animals.
Nils was directed to sit in the carriage, and after a
few minutes Kazi appeared with his two personal
guards. He was naked as before, except for jew-
elled harness and an immense sword and dagger,
and rode standing, grim-faced and cold, a huge
obscene satyr figure preceded and followed by a
roar of orc voices in the street and a great surge of
emotion that Nils read as an overwhelming broth
of fear, adoration and hopelessness.

The large stone structure was a stadium. The open
ground around it had row upon row of hitching
posts, where thousands of horses stood in a haze of
dust raised by hundreds more being ridden into
the area by horse barbarians.

The arena itself was an oval of about forty by
seventy meters, encircled by a wall five meters
high. Around it rose tier upon tier of seats rapidly
filling with armed men. The north-facing side,
which held the royal box, was clearly reserved for
orcs; the rest of it held horse barbarians. Kazi's
throne was on a low pedestal. To each side, slightly
ahead and a half-meter lower, were several other
upholstered seats, obviously for guests. Only one
was occupied, by Nils. Behind Nils and next to
him stood Kazi's two personal guards. Others of
the elite guard stood around the perimeter of the
box.

Near one end of the field was a stone pillar eight
or ten meters high, topped by an open platform.

Squatting chained on the platform was a large beast, a troll, deformed, with a great hump on its back and one arm that was only partially developed, ending in a single hooked finger. A man stood beside it.

Kazi looked at it through Nils's eyes, and his question entered Nils's mind without having been verbalized.

"It's a troll," Nils answered. "I was told it's probably a species brought from the stars by the ancients."

"Your teacher was an astute man." Kazi turned his own eyes toward the grotesque. "By nature it's a hunter, broadcasting terror vocally and psionically to confuse its prey. This one comes from inbreeding a voiceless mutant strain, and is only able to echo and amplify emotions that it senses around it. The man beside it is a psi, who directs its attention to the victims in the arena so the spectators can fully enjoy their fear and agony. It's one of the greatest emotional experiences possible to them."

"Can trolls be used as fighters?" Nils asked.

"No. Even from carefully selected breeding stock they proved too stupid, and they terrify the soldiers." Kazi turned and looked steadily at and into Nils. "None of this seems to disturb you. We'll see how you like the exhibitions; there may be hope for you yet."

The seats were nearly full now; only a trickle of men still moved in the aisles. Nils believed nearly all of the men Nephthys had mentioned must be in the stadium. Kazi stood, raising an arm and sending a psi command. Trumpeters at the parapet raised long brass horns and blew, the high, clear note belling loud even in the uppermost seats.

At one end of the arena a gate opened. Four very tall, slender man, almost black, strode onto the field, the gate closing behind them. The troll immediately picked up their emotions—uncertainty, caution, a contained fear. They were naked and unarmed. A single trumpet blew, and a gate opened at the other end of the field. Ten tiny figures trotted out, no larger than children. Each carried a stabbing spear about as long as himself, fastened to his wrist by a chain. The troll's mind turned for a moment to the pygmies and poured out their cold, implacable hatred for the tall persecutors of their race, then picked up the shock of recognition and alarm from the victims.

The pygmies consulted for a moment and then formed a row, trotting toward the tall men, who separated, two running toward each side of the oval. Instantly the pygmy line turned toward two of them. One continued running along the base of the wall. The other turned toward the closed gate, and the line followed him. His fear turned to desperation as he saw himself singled out, and his long legs flashed as he tried to run around them. The crowd experienced his dismay as he was cut off, and he stopped, spun, doubled back and stopped again. Then he took several driving steps directly toward the pygmies and hurdled high, clearing the nearest by a meter, but a broad blade stabbed upward and the flash of shock and terror almost drowned out the flame of pain in his groin and lower abdomen.

The next tall black that the pygmies singled out was a different cut of man. Cornered, he feinted, drawing a thrust from the nearest pygmy. With an explosion of savage joy he grabbed the shaft of the spear, spun, and jerked the tiny man off his feet, snapping the chain. But he was armed too late. Another spear sliced across the back of his ribs and sank into his upper arm. His surge of rage and frustration filled the stadium as he spun again, slashing and stabbing, and went down beneath a flurry of thrusts.

During the melee another of the tall blacks had rushed into the rear of the pygmies, striking with a calloused foot driven by a long sinewy thigh, killing pouring from him, and when he went down, he had broken two small necks.

The remaining tall man stood near the center of the arena, watching the five surviving pygmies trot toward him. His mind was fogged with fear, unable to function. For a moment the troll was tuned again to the hunters, and the crowd sensed that they intended to play with the last victim. He broke then and ran toward the wall. His leap upward was a prodigy of strength, but his fingers found only smooth stone. He fell to the sand and knelt with his forearms across his face, paralyzed. The pygmies killed him quickly in disgust, and the crowd roared.

A gate opened, and after a moment's hesitation they trotted out of sight, while a cart rolled across the sand and the bodies were thrown into it. Meanwhile, two men with spades dug a hole in the middle of the arena.

When the cart had left, the trumpets blew again. A horse walked into the arena dragging a post. Spiked to it and braced were two cross pieces, a large X with a man spread-eagled on it, robust and hairy. The post was hoisted, dropped into the hole and tamped into place.

"An officer of mine," Kazi commented, "with a mind given to disloyal fantasies."

The man hung there in the bright sunshine, and his amplified emotion was a roiling cloud of hate that filled the stadium. A single trumpet sounded and two men walked onto the sand, followed by two others with a small chest fitted with carrying poles. They came from the gate that the victim faced, and the crowd felt his grim recognition and the defiance and determination that followed.

The two men were artists, and defiance and hatred were quickly displaced. At informal affairs they might have made him last for hours, for he had a constitution like a bull, but now they had a schedule to keep, and their purpose was a maximum of agony and emotional degradation while time trickled in tiny white grains through the narrow waist of their glass.

When the sand was cleared again, four robed and hooded figures were led out by a soldier. Two men with megaphones followed.

"They are members of a religious sect," Kazi's mind remarked to Nils, "with very strong superstitions and taboos. This will appeal especially to my orcs."

Each man with a megaphone explained in two languages what would happen. At each recitation some part of the crowd burst into coarse laughter. The emotional pickup indicated that the women understood the last language. The crowd waited expectantly and again the single trumpet blew. Kazi leaned forward intently.

The initial flood of shock and loathing that the

troll had echoed dropped to a low wash of almost unbearable fascination and dread that gripped the crowd for slow moments, swelling gradually and holding them silent. Then their minds were torn by pain and shrill terror. The guard beside Nils was staring forward, oblivious to anything but the spectacle, his sword arm bent rigidly, his knuckles tight. Nils rose, thrusting back hard with an elbow into the man's groin as he turned, grabbing the sword wrist with steel fingers. He tore the sword from the man's agony-loosened grip and thrust it into the guard on the step behind him. The disarmed guard beside him, though half-doubled and gasping with pain, wrapped burly arms around Nils's waist and lunged forward, throwing him against the throne pedestal.

In that moment Kazi became aware and turned. In a shock of surprised fear he struck wildly but powerfully with a huge fist. A metallic taste, and blackness, filled Nils's head as he fell sideways and lay still.

Nils awoke from the wetness of a pail of water thrown on him. His hands were tied behind him, and the side of his aching face lay on packed sand foul with the smell of animal urine. He heard the muffled sound of trumpets, and rough hands pulled him upright to send him stumbling through a gate into the dazzling brightness of the arena. Bars closed behind him and a voice growled in Anglic to back up to them so that his bonds could be cut. He did. A short sword was tossed between the bars and he picked it up. Glancing back, he saw three bowmen standing behind the gate with arrows nocked on sinews.

His loose pantaloons and robe were gone. Moving
out of line with the gate, Nils stayed close to the
wall, waiting. The troll found only a high calm to
echo, and the crowd, after a moment, began to
murmur in puzzlement.

A single trumpet blew.

Four great wild dogs came through the opposite
gate. They stood for a moment, dazzled and confused by the bright sunlight and the chaos of sounds
and smells, then saw him and approached at a
tentative trot.

Nils stood relaxed and waiting, and the dogs
stopped a dozen meters away. They were hungry
but also curious and wary, for they had never
encountered a man who acted like this one. The
largest sat down on the sand, facing Nils, tongue
lolling, and the crowd began to grumble. The dogs
looked up toward the noise and anger, forgetting
for a moment the curiosity on the sand before
them. Things began to land around them—iron
knuckles, knives, even helmets. Suddenly the leader
stood, teeth bared, hackles raised, looking up into
the stands. From behind the bars arrows hummed,
striking deeply, and the beasts lay jerking or dead,
making bloody patches on the sand.

Then nothing. The sun burned down. Nils waited
silently and at ease while the stands murmured.
Somewhere someone was improvising. At length a
single trumpet blew again, and a gate opened. A
male lion trotted out, in his prime and unfed, and
like the dogs stood dazzled for a moment. His
gaze settled on the dead dogs, perhaps drawn there
by the smell of blood, and then moved to the
solitary man. Nils touched its mind and found
hunger and anger. It stood for a moment, tail

switching from side to side, then stalked slowly
across the sand. Still the troll echoed no fear, and
the crowd watched fascinated. Thirty meters away
the lion stopped for a long moment, tail lashing
now, staring at the man before it, then suddenly
rushed forward with shocking speed. Nils crouched,
not knowing whether it would spring or simply
charge into him. At the last instant he threw himself sideways, twisting and striking as he fell away.
The lion struck the wall and turned, snarling, a
wound pouring blood from the side of its neck,
and a cheer arose from the stands.

Nils had landed in a crouch, but had barely set
himself when the lion moved toward him again, at
close quarters now, boxing at him with a huge and
deadly paw. It was a feint so quick that Nils did
not have time to be drawn out before the animal
lunged at him. Nils sprang back, striking again,
the sword laying back the flesh of the lion's cheek
and jaw so that for an instant it recoiled, and Nils
attacked, striking again and again in an astonish-
ing fury that stunned the stands. The lion fell to its
side with a broken sword in its skull, its sinewy
body and hindquarters flexing and jerking, while
Nils's arm chopped twice more with a bladeless
hilt.

He stood then, chest heaving and sweat dripping
from the charge of energy that had surged through
him, stunned by the simple fact of life, while the
stands came apart with noise. He realized that he
was not even scratched, and stood calmly again,
the tremor fading from his hands and knees, waiting weaponless for what would come next.

*   *   *

He didn't wait long. When the third trumpet blew, a narrow gate opened and an orc officer entered the arena. Tall, muscular, he strode several paces out onto the sand, then stood grinning around at the stands and brandishing his sword overhead. From the orcs there rose a storm of cheers and whistles that drowned out the murmurs and scattered hoots from the seats on the other side. The troll focused its psi sense on the mind of the sinewy, sun-bronzed orc, broadcasting the sadistic anticipation it found there. Then it gave its attention to Nils, where it found only watchfulness. The orc was still fifteen meters away when a barbarian in the stand threw a long curved sword at Nils's feet. He pounced on it and, as quickly as the lion, charged at the startled officer. For a moment steel clashed against steel while the crowd roared. But only for a moment. Nils's blade sliced through neck and chest, shearing ribs like brittle sticks, the force of the blow driving the man to his knees and carrying Nils off-balance so that he staggered and caught himself on one hand in the blood-slimed sand. He looked at it and arose, grim and fearsome, above the nearly bisected corpse.

And the cheers died. Kazi stood dark and terrible in his box, holding the troll's mind with his like a club—buffeting the crowd with his rage until they huddled cold with shock and fear . . . orc and barbarian alike. He turned to Nils then, and in that instant Nils struck with his own mind, through the lens of the troll, a shaft of pure deadliness that he had not known he had, so that Kazi staggered back and fell, consciousness suddenly blacked out by the overload.

Men lay sprawled against each other in the stands

or sat slumped, stupefied. Nils sprinted to the gate and reached a brawny forearm between two bars to grasp and turned the heavy bolt latch. He stepped across the tangle of archers while a burly orc sat slumped against a wall, staring dully at him. Nils traded sheathless sword for the orc's harness and weapons. Sensing the return of awareness in the man he ran him through, then loped across the chamber and up a ramp. The unlocked gate at its end yielded easily to his pull and he was in a concrete chute that led into the open. He loped up that and climbed a gate. A few horse barbarians were outside, none near, moving uncertainly through the rows of horses or staring up at the stands. Nils could sense the slow return of consciousness behind him. Dropping to the dusty ground, he sauntered casually in among the nervous stamping horses, careful to avoid being kicked.

Near the outer edge of the horse park he chose a powerful stallion whose great haunches would not tire quickly under his weight. Standing before it, he tuned to its simple, nervous mind, holding its bridle and stroking its velvety nose until it stood calmly, eyes on him and ears forward. Then he stepped beside it, reached for the stirrup with a foot, and hoisted himself easily into the saddle.

It guided much like a Swedish pony, but it was much more—the mount of a chief of horse barbarians—and Nils urged it into an easy trot down a broad, dusty lane separating the camps of two Turkish tribes.

16.

The sun was a red ball hanging two fingers above the horizon. When the guard on a gate tower could no longer see its blood-colored upper rim, he would blow a horn and that gate would be closed.

The road outside the south gate of Pest was crowded with peasants on foot and in carts, and a few horsemen, leaving the city while the gate was still open. A smaller number struggled against the current to enter. An impatient merchant threatened them with the bulk and hooves of his big gelding, striking occasionally with his quirt at some peasant head as he pushed his way, cursing, through the crowd. Just ahead of him a huge peasant in a ragged cloak half turned and, taking the bridle in a large, thick hand, slowed the horse. Incensed at the impertinence, the merchant stood in his stirrups, quirt raised. The blue eyes that met his neither threatened nor feared; if anything, they were mildly interested and perhaps very slightly amused. Reddening, the merchant sat down again, to be led through the gate at the pace of a peasant walking in a crowd.

A little inside the gate, Nils let go the bridle and turned down the first side street that circled inside the city. He had several purposes: kill Ahmed, tell Janos what had happened to Imre, and take Ahmed's psi tuner. But it would be dangerous to try to enter the palace until Ahmed was asleep. The man's psi was remarkably sensitive and alert, and he had henchmen in Janos's guard, one of them a psi. If he detected Nils either directly or through the mind of someone who saw and recognized him, he could be expected to act instantly to have the northman murdered.

Walking the streets was as good a way as any to kill time until Ahmed should have retired.

Pest was a very large town for its time, with a wall eight kilometers around. The narrow, cobbled outer street was walled on each side by two-storied buildings broken only by intersecting streets and an occasional small courtyard or dark and narrow passage. Most of the buildings were dwellings— some tenements and some the homes of merchants or artisans with their places of business. Near each of the city gates the dwellings gave way to taverns, inns and stables. There the night air was heavy with the pungency of horses and hay, the rancid odor of dried urine from walls and cobblestones, and the faint residual sweet-sour smell of last night's vomit.

Nils took a slow two hours to walk around the outer street and was approaching the gate by which he had entered, when several knights came out of a tavern. They were at the stage of the evening when their inhibitions, never the strongest, were negligible, but their coordination was not yet seriously impaired. The smallest of them, oblivious to everything but the gesture-filled story he was telling, almost walked into Nils in the semi-darkness of the street, then suddenly recoiled from the near collision.

"Peasant swine! Watch where you're going!"

"Excuse me, sir, I meant no harm."

The knight's eyes narrowed. Truly a very big peasant. "Excuse you? You almost walked into me, you stupid clod." His sword was in his hand. "I *may* excuse you at that, though, if you get down on your knees and beg nicely enough."

The knights had surrounded Nils now, each with drawn sword. He sensed a severe beating here, with injuries possibly serious, unless he did something to forestall it. He began to kneel, slowly and clumsily, then lunged forward, left hand clutching the sword wrist of his accoster, his right crushing the knight's nose and upper mandible as he charged over him. Stumbling on the falling knight, Nils caught himself on one hand and sprang forward again to flee, but the point of a wildly swung sword sliced one buttock deeply.

Even so, within fifty meters the knights gave up the chase. But in the intersection just ahead was a patrol of wardens, bows bent. One let go an arrow at Nils's belly. Reacting instantly, he dodged and ran on a few paces, another arrow driving almost through his thick left thigh. He stopped, nearly falling, aware that if he didn't, the other wardens would surely shoot him down. The knights behind him came on again, and Nils turned to face them.

"Wait!" one shouted. "I know this man."

And now Nils knew him, not by his appearance, for he had shaved his beard and wore jerkin and hose, but by the picture in the man's mind. He had been one of Lord Lajos's border patrol that had intercepted Nils on the river ice when he had first entered Hungary.

"You heard the clod talk," the knight said. "He's a foreigner. I remember him by his size and yellow hair. The one who escaped from the dungeon last year and killed several of the guards doing it."

"That one! Let's finish him."

"No!" The man who had recognized Nils grabbed the other by the arm. "He's worth many forints to us alive. We can take him to the palace and have him put in the dungeon for attacking a knight. He won't escape this time—not in the shape he's in. Then we'll send word to Lord Lajos. He'll want the foreigner, and he's the king's guest. The king will oblige, and you can bet that Lajos will pay us all well."

Quickly they threw Nils to the cobblestones, pushed the head of the arrow out through the back of the thickly muscled leg, and broke the shaft in front of the feathers. Then they pulled it out and stuffed pieces of his rags into the hole to slow the flow of blood.

Ahmed sat straight and intent at his desk. There could be no doubt about it; the prisoner just brought into the palace was the big barbarian, and his friends in the palace guard would not be happy about it. He had better act now. Opening a little chest on his desk he took out a sheet of parchment and hurried from the room.

Nils lay in a cell neither shackled nor locked in. One of the guard knelt beside him cleaning the wound with big, careful hands. Nils's calm gray face showed no interest in the sudden commotion down the passageway.

"The King!" a voice shouted.

"That'll do it," said the guard, standing. "He'll get you out of here."

But Nils did not sit up. He saw the king's mind clearly.

In a moment Janos stood before the cell, his voice grim with hate. "You filth! You swine! The boy would have given you almost anything, but you wanted what he would not give—his decency." Janos turned to the physician who had hurried, wheezing, behind him. "See that he's able to walk again by the next holiday. I want him to walk to the gallows. And I want him strong enough to take a long time to choke—he'll learn how Imre felt being strangled."

For a moment more he glared at Nils, then turned and walked swiftly away.

Janos stood at his window, staring unseeingly into the early June dawn. In his grief and bitterness he had not slept. Yet he was past the peak of it and could think again. He had liked his big barbarian guard and had never sensed his weakness. But you couldn't know what a barbarian might do.

There was a rap on his chamber door. He turned. "Yes?"

A guard opened it apologetically. "I could hear you moving around, Your Highness, and knew you were awake. Sergeant Bela would like to talk to you."

"At this hour? What about?"

"The barbarian, Your Highness."

The king stared at him with narrowed eyes. "All right, let him in. But you and Sandor stay with us."

Bela was ushered in and dropped immediately to one knee. The words began to pour out. "Your Highness, I've heard what has been said about the barbarian—what you have been told. And I've talked to him." Without a pause he told about the friendship between Nils and Imre, their joking closeness, of being with them continously on the barge and of his farewell to them in the City of Kazi. "And Your Highness, I know it's not true. He couldn't have been that way without some of us seeing some sign of it and speaking of it. He just couldn't have done it. It would be impossible for him. He says that Kazi himself had Imre killed, on a whim. And it's true, Your Highness; I know it. By my life I swear he is telling the truth!"

"Shut up!" shouted Janos. "By your life, eh? Guards, take this lunatic out of here and lock him up." The shaken guards put the points of their swords to Bela's chest, and he stood.

"I swear it, Your Highness," Bela said in little more than a whisper. "Nils is telling the truth. He doesn't know how to lie."

The door of Ahmed's chamber opened quietly and Janos' two guards stepped in and to the side. The king entered behind them and walked up to the cot of the sleeping Sudanese. Drawing back the blanket he placed his dagger point at Ahmed's throat, laying his hand on the dark arched brow so the man would not lift his head abruptly.

"Ahmed. Wake up."

Ahmed awoke fully alert at the words and knew

his danger instantly. He touched the mind of his own bodyguard, fading in death outside his door. The king's mind was cold and hard, and he knew that this time it could not be cozened.

"You said the letter came yesterday. Why didn't you show it to me until tonight?"

"As I said, Highness, I couldn't bring myself to give it to you at first. I knew how terrible the news would be for you."

"Liar! You have never had a merciful thought. And why did Kazi send it to you instead of to me?"

Never a merciful thought. He is almost right, Ahmed realized. Not for many years. The Sudanese was suddenly tired and didn't particularly care what happened to him, but he answered anyway, sensing it would do no good.

"He sent it to me so that I could use my judgement as to whether or when to give it to you."

The king's eyes were slitted, his grim face pale in the dawn light. "The barbarian has said that Kazi had the boy killed. How do you answer that?"

"The barbarian lies."

Janos' voice dropped to a hoarse undertone. "And do you remember what you told me after you first looked into his mind, early last winter?"

Ahmed simply looked at the king, too tired to answer. He felt the mind explode at him in the same instant the blade plunged in, watched in dim and heavy apathy as his body first stiffened, then slowly relaxed. It . . . could . . . not . . .

Tears of release and grief washed down the king's cheeks as he spoke to the dark corpse. "You said he didn't lie—that he wasn't able to lie. Now I know who the liars were, and have been all along, and I sent my son, the boy who was like a son to me, to be killed by him."

He turned to his guards, who stood with their jaws hanging in gross astonishment. "Get this carrion out of here," he rasped. And pointing to the corpse of Ahmed he added, "And see that that one is fed to the swine."

17.

Early in the morning, under the fussy directions of the asthmatic physician, the strong hands of guards lifted Nils onto a litter and carried him from the dungeon to a softer bed. He gave them almost no attention, for he was busy using a skill Ilse had taught him. He was healing his body.

Ilse was aware of the cellular structure of tissues—the Kinfolk had maintained all they could of ancient knowledge—and the circulation of the blood was known by everyone. That knowledge was not very functional, though, in the sense that she could do much with it. It served mainly to provide a sense of understanding. But the body itself understands the body much better than any physiologist ever had. The ability her father had developed and taught her was the ability to impose conscious purpose on autonomic physiological processes.

Therefore, Nils didn't try to think of a cell or a tissue. He simply fixed his attention totally on a whole and undamaged thigh and buttock, with a completeness of concentration that Ilse had developed through disciplined practice but that he had mastered almost as quickly as the possibility had been demonstrated to him.

Although his eyes were closed, his other senses received the thoughts, sounds, smells and touches that encountered them. But in his trancelike concentration, that part of him which screened sensory data for referral to action centers or to the higher level analytical center, operated on a basis of passing only emergency messages.

The physician sat beside him, aware that the wisest thing to do was nothing. For despite the profoundness of Nils's trance, he clearly was not in a coma. His breathing was deep and regular, his brow neither hot nor cold, and his heartbeat was strong.

Beginning about midday Nils awakened periodically for water and nourishment. After eating lightly and drinking, he would return to his healing trance.

By early on the fourth day healing was far advanced, and Nils walked with Janos to Ahmed's chamber. A servant with hammer and chisel broke the hasp on the chest they found there. Nils opened it, took out a gray plastic boxed stamped with the meaningless symbols:

PROP INST MENTAL PHEN
UNIV TEL AVIV

and flipped the switch.

The instruments once used for "finding" other tuners had used electricity and had long since been inoperable and lost. Without knowing the setting of a particular tuner there was no real possiblity of tuning to it. Nils's memory was precise, however; he set the coarse tuning, then the fine, and then the microtuner. Finally, carefully, he set the vernier. Then he looked at the number stamped on the case and held in his mind the clear picture of a series of digits: 37-02-103-8. He waited for several moments. It was the time of day when members of the Inner Circle communicated.

"Nils!" Raadgiver had recognized his mind. The wait had been the time necessary to duplicate the setting Nils's mind had held for him. "Where are you, Nils? And what set is that? I've never heard of that number before."

Nils reran the audio-visual sequence of relevant events for Raadgiver's mind, beginning with the ambush in the Bavarian forest.

Raadgiver digested the information for a few moments and then began. Kazi had begun his invasion, landing his army from a fleet of ships on the north coast of the Black Sea. His advance forces had easily broken the resistance of local Ukrainian nobles. The Inner Circle had a substantial picture of events. One of the Wandering Kin, with a psi tuner, had been sent from the court of Saxony to King Vlad of the South Ukraine in the expectation that Kazi would strike there first.

In spite of the atrocities being committed, Vlad was not seriously trying to defend his kingdom, which was mostly open steppe. Instead he was pulling back his army of nearly four thousand knights to join with Nikolas of the North Ukraine, numbering about twenty-five hundred. They hoped to make a stand in the northwest, where the grasslands were interspersed with forest, providing an opportunity for a cavalry guerrilla and the prospect of help from the neighboring Poles.

"The best army in Kazi's way," Raadgiver continued, "is that of Casimir of Poland. It has been a curse to the Balts, the Ukrainians, the Saxons and

Prussians for years, and when fully gathered, it numbers perhaps six thousand. Most important, it is disciplined and well led. Casimir is gathering it now, and the Prussians and Saxons are gathering theirs. We have spread the word everywhere.

"But now there is another invasion, in northern Poland, by the northmen, your own people. There are still only a few, perhaps two hundred, holding a tiny area on the coast, but their position is impossible to attack on horseback because of marshes, and a force of knights sent against them on foot was routed. And more are expected, for they have stolen several Polish and Danish ships.

"When enough have landed they will surely try to break out of the section they hold now, so Casimir is sending a strong army that will attack them when they move. And the King of Prussia is holding his army to fight them, too. And by holding these armies from joining with the Ukrainians, the neovikings are destroying what little chance we have against Kazi."

Raadgiver read the question in Nils's mind. "It was the winter that caused it," the counselor explained. "In Denmark it was the worst ever. In the northlands it was so bad that your tribes felt they would hardly survive another. We captured several wounded when Norsk raiders took a Danish ship, and I questioned them and read their minds. The three tribes have joined in this and plan to move all their people before winter if they can.

"It's not northern Poland they're interested in. They hope to cross the continent to the Mediterranean. They'll never make it, of course; all of them together are far too few. They underestimate the Poles and the Germans. But they are weakening us at a critical time."

Nils interrupted. "Who is their war chief?"

"A man called Scar Belly."

"Ah, Björn Ärrbuk! I would rather fight the troll again, or even the lion. And he is the greatest raid leader of the Svear, as my clan has learned by experience. You would take the tribes more seriously if you knew him better.

"Now, listen to me; this is very important. The tribes can be your salvation instead of your ruin, if they are led against Kazi. But you'll have to keep war from starting between the Poles and the tribes—keep them from wasting one another. For the tribes do what few armies do. They fight on foot more than on horseback, and stealth and cunning are their pride.

"Once you told me that one of the Inner Circle, a Jan Reszke, was counselor to Casimir. Is he still?"

"Yes."

"Good. Tell him I'm coming north to turn the tribes eastward against Kazi. Tell him to keep Casimir from attacking them. Have him urge Casimir to send as many troops as possible against Kazi."

"Are you telling me you can get the tribes to abandon their plans and follow you against Kazi? You're only a youth, and an outcast at that."

"We have a legend in the north," Nils answered. "Once, when the tribes were younger, the Jötar made war on the Svear, and the Jötar were stronger so that it seemed they would destroy and enslave the other tribes. But then a young warrior arose among the Svear who became a raid leader and led several brilliant raids. In one they surprised and killed the chief of the Jötar and several of their clan chieftains.

"This demoralized the Jötar and heartened the Svear, so that the tide was turned. And then the young warrior disappeared, but in their successes no one missed him. For several years the Svear prevailed, burning villages and haystacks and destroying cattle, as the Jötar had before them, until it appeared it was the Jötar who would be destroyed and enslaved.

"And then a young warrior among the Jötar was made a raid leader and led a daring raid which left the chief of the Svear dead, along with several of their principal raid leaders. It was then that both tribes realized this was the same youth who had saved the Svear earlier, but until he wanted them to, they had not been able to recognize him, because he was a wizard. And he said he was not of any clan or tribe but was simply a northman.

"Then he called a council of all the warriors of the three tribes, and they came without weapons, as he told them. And in the council he put before them the bans, and after they had counciled with one another they approved them. They would still fight, for that was their nature, but they would not take each other's land. They could kill men, but not women or children. They could not burn barns or dwellings, but only longhouses. They could burn straw stacks, but not hay stacks. They could steal livestock, but they could not kill what they could not drive away. And they could kill in vengeance only for specified wrongs and within approved feuds.

"And all the clans agreed to this and praised the young warrior, and all the warriors lined up to

honor him and clasp his hand. But one warrior
hated him because he did not want to change, so
he hid a small poisoned knife in his breeches. And
when he came up to him, he struck him with it,
killing him.

"Then, instead of making a burial mound, they
put the body in a canoe and let it float on the
river, although they didn't know why. And it floated
down the river to the sea and out of sight.

"And then they realized that no one knew his
name, so they called him The Yngling. I know that,
in Danish, yngling means a youth, a youngling.
But among the tribes it has not been so used since,
for it can only be used as his name.

"Although some of the details are fanciful, the
story is basically true, history as well as legend.
And the tribes believe that The Yngling will come
again in a time of great need. Maybe this is the
time."

For several seconds Raadgiver's mind framed
no response, and when it did, it was through a
sense of disorientation and some unease. His skin
crawled. "I will send one of the Wandering Kin to
them, a Dane who has been in Jötmark. He will be
able to talk to them. But will they believe?"

"Most will neither believe nor disbelieve. But
that isn't important. What is important is that
they will watch for me, prepared to listen. Can
you give me the name of one of the kinfolk near
Pest, and how I can find him?"

Nils followed Raadgiver's mind while the counselor looked into the ledger where he kept the
names and whereabouts of the more settled kin, as
best he knew them. His eyes stopped at a name
and location for Nils to read.

"Good. Here is what I'll do before I start north. The Magyars are good fighters, well mounted. I'll send them northeast over the mountains to join the Poles and Ukrainians. Let the Poles and Ukrainians know this. And if your psi, Zoltan Kossuth, is willing and able to go with them, I'll give him this psi tuner. That will give the Magyars contact with the others. He'll get in touch with you later for the settings of any tuners you think he should contact."

I *will lead the tribes against Kazi.* I *will send the Magyars.* A weakness, a gray fear, began to settle over Raadgiver. In his long life he had heard big boasts and hollow promises, had even been privy to the minds of megalomaniacs. But those, he told himself, had not been men on whom so much depended. Yet his fear had grown from more than that, and less, grown from something inside *him* that he did not see, could not look at. Nils's thoughts had seemed insane, but yet they had a sense of certainty and the feel of clear and powerful sanity. And that was impossible. That *was* insane. The old psi's stable data were dissolving, the keystones of his personal world.

Nils helped him on both counts with a new and simple stable datum, putting it out as if the thought were Raadgiver's own, and the man took it. *This is the* New Man, *maturing. Who knows what* He *can do?* The weakness fell away, replaced by hope.

"Is there anything more you have to tell me?" Nils asked.

"Nothing more," Raadgiver replied.

They saluted each other and Nils replaced the tuner in the chest.

*   *   *

During the long, voiceless conversation Janos had begun to grow irritated, understanding only that Nils was sitting there silently ignoring him. But he had not interrupted. When it was over, Nils turned.

"Your Highness," he said, "I can do what Ahmed did. I can look into minds and speak without sound to others like me. This—" he gestured to where he had replaced the tuner—"is a means by which two like me can speak to one another with the mind, at great distances. Ahmed was not only a counselor loaned to you. He was also a spy against you, reporting everything to Kazi through this. I was using it now to speak with my teacher on the shore of the northern sea."

There was a copy of an ancient topographic map of Europe on the wall, with the modern states outlined on it. Nils walked over to it. "About here is where Kazi's army is now, with thirty thousand men," he said pointing. "The Ukrainians are far too few to hold him, even if the Poles arrive soon to help. But if you took your army over the mountains, here, your combined forces could delay and damage him until other kings can gather theirs."

Janos frowned. "But Kazi's army is more powerful than all the others put together. Otherwise, I'd never have allied myself with him."

"That's what he wanted you to believe," Nils answered. "And in open battle it would be true. But in that land you could work as small units, striking and then running to cover to strike again elsewhere."

Janos' face sharpened. "And who asked your

advice?" he said coldly. "Have you forgotten that you're a foreigner of common blood?"

Nils grinned. "I'm young but not foolish, Your Highness. Yet I do indeed advise," he continued more seriously. "And deep in your mind you know my advice is good, because if you don't combine armies, Kazi will eat you up separately. But you are a king, used to listening to advice only when you've asked for it, and so my boldness offended you. Yet I'm only a foreigner, a commoner, a barbarian, and a mere youth to boot. You wouldn't have asked for my advice, so I had to give it uninvited."

The king stared at Nils for several seconds before a smile began to break his scowl. "You're a scoundrel, barbarian," he said, clapping the warrior's shoulder. "But allowances must be made for barbarians, at least for those who are giants and great swordsmen who can look into the minds of others and speak across half a world and heal dirty wounds in three days. You're right. We must move, for better or for worse, and if need be we'll die like men, with swords in our hands. And you will come with us, and I'll continue to listen to your unasked-for advice."

"Highness," said Nils, suddenly solemn, "with your permission I'll go instead to my own people and lead them against Kazi. They are not numerous, but they fight with a savagery and cunning that will warm your blood to see."

"All right, all right," the king said, shaking his head ruefully. "I bow to your will again. If your people are all like you, they can probably talk Kazi into surrender."

*　　*　　*

Janos sent riders ordering the nobles to gather at the palace on the sixth day, which was as soon as the more distant could possibly arrive if they left at once. The orders specified foreign danger to the realm, in order that there would be no delaying by independent lords who might otherwise be inclined to frustrate him.

After two more days spent resting and healing, Nils submitted his newly knitted thigh and hip to a saddle and rode a ferry across the Duna to the town of Buda. He didn't want to send a messenger to Zoltan Kossuth, the psi, in case the request be interpreted as an invitation to a trap.

Nils led his horse off the ferry and spoke to a dockman. "Where can I find the inn of Zoltan Kossuth?" he asked.

"Would that be the Zoltan Kossuth who is called the Bear? Turn left on the outer street. His is the inn just past the South Gate, under the sign of the bear, and the stable next to it is his, too. It's the best inn in town, if you like your inns orderly. The Bear is notorious for throwing out troublemakers with his own tender hands, although"—he sized Nils up with a leer more gaps than teeth—"He'd have his hands more than full trying to throw you out. Not that I'm calling you a troublemaker, you understand, but if you were."

Nils grinned back, mounted, and started down the cobbled street. "And the fare is good for both man and horse," the dockman shouted after him.

Nils strode into the inn, which was quiet at that hour. The keeper was talking with two men who were telling him more than they realized. Tuned for it, Nils had detected the man's psi before reaching the stable, but engrossed as the Bear was in the words and thoughts he was listening to, he wasn't aware of Nils until the barbarian came through the door.

Zoltan Kossuth was not admired for his beauty. His round head had no hair above the ears, but his black beard, clipped somewhat short, grew densely to the eye sockets, and a similar but untrimmed growth bushed out obstreperously through gaps in the front of a shirt that had more than it could do to contain an enormous chest. He was of moderate height, but his burly hundred kilos made him look stubby. Just for a moment he glanced up balefully at the strange psi, then seeing a servant move to wait on Nils, he returned to his conversation.

Nils sat in an inner corner nursing an ale and a bowl of dry beef. He felt no need to interrupt the Bear's conversation, but saw no point in waiting needlessly if the innkeeper's interest in it was not serious. Therefore, he held in his mind for a moment a clear picture of the Bear holding a gray plastic psi tuner, at the same time naming it in case the Bear would not recognize one by sight.

Zoltan Kossuth scowled across at Nils, excused himself from the table and disappeared into a back room. "Who are you and what do you want?" he demanded mentally.

"I am Nils Järnhann, on business of the Inner Circle and the king."

This alarmed the Bear. Covering his intentions and actions with discursive camouflage, he walked to a crossbow hanging on the wall. "I'm not aware that a king of Hungary has had dealings with one of the Inner Circle since old Mihaly, counselor to Janos I, was murdered by an agent of Baalzebub when I was a boy." The Bear cranked the crossbow and set a dart to it. "What I would like to know is how you can be on business which is of both the Inner Circle and of Janos III."

"Put down your weapon, Innkeeper." And Nils ran through his mind a rapid montage of Kazi, of Kazi's guard lopping off the head of Imre Rakosi, and of vile acts in the arena. And the identities of all were clear, although Zoltan Kossuth had not known what Kazi looked like until that moment. And it was clear, too, what Nils's mission had been. Then the picture was of Janos leaning over a cot, slicing open the throat of Ahmed.

The innkeeper was a suspicious man for someone who could read minds, but he accepted this intuitively. Removing the dart, he pulled the trigger with a twang and hung up the crossbow. "And what do you want of me?" he asked.

When Nils was finished at the inn, he resaddled his horse and left Buda through the West Gate, riding leisurely toward the castle of Lord Miklos, which domintaed the town from a nearby hill. Miklos was the town's protector, deriving an important part of his wealth from its tribute. Prairie flowers bloomed along the climbing dusty road, and the moat surrounding the castle was green with the spears of new cattail leaves that had crowded through the broken blades and stalks of last year's growth. The shallow water, already thick with algae, lost as much to the sun in dry weather as it gained from the overflow of the castle's spring and the waste that emptied into it through an odorous concrete pipe.

The countryside was at peace, the drawbridge down, and the gatekeepers at ease. "Who are you, stranger, and what is your business here?" one called genially as Nils drew up his horse at the outer end.

"I want to speak to Lord Miklos. My name is Nils."

The man's mind told Nils that he might not remember such an outlandish name long enough to repeat it to his master's page.

"Tell him it's the big barbarian he rescued from Lord Lajos' castle," Nils added.

A grin split the guard's brawl-sculptured face and he saluted Nils before he turned to carry the message. The ill-feeling between the two nobles was shared by their retainers.

Lord Miklos was sitting on a stool, stripped to the waist, when Nils was ushered into his chamber. One servant was washing the nobleman's feet and ankles while another towelled his still lean torso. "Ah-ha, it *is* you. Sit down, my friend. I've been in the fields this morning inspecting the work, and that's a dirty occupation in such dry weather. I'm afraid our talk will have to be short, as my vassals are waiting to meet with me at the noon meal. For buiness. Have you come to join my guard?" He eyed Nils's expensive clothes.

"No, m' Lord." Nils looked at the servants and spoke in Anglic. "I have news for your ears alone."

The old knight straightened and spoke to the servants, who speeded their work and left. "What is it?" he asked.

"I've come to tell you of the king and Baalzebub, but there's quite a bit of it and it will take time. Also, it's best if King Janos doesn't learn about my visit here."

"Plague and death!" Miklos strode to a bell cord

and pulled it. In a moment a page entered. "Lad, I don't want to be disturbed until I ring again. Tell my guests I'll be delayed. Tell the steward to hold the meal ... no, tell him to feed the guests. I'll come later."

The page left and Miklos turned to Nils. "All right, my big friend, tell me everything."

Speaking Magyar, Nils told him of Kazi the Conqueror who was the basis in fact for Baalzebub, of Kazi's military strength and psi power and of his intention to conquer Europe.

"And you say this creature has lived since ancient times and looks into men's minds?"

"Yes. And there are others who can read thoughts," Nils answered. "I'm one of them." Without giving Miklos time to react fully to that, Nils told him of Janos' visit to Kazi's city some years earlier, of his conviction that Kazi could not be withstood and of his decision to ally himself to Kazi when the time came to assume the throne of Hungary. Then, without being specific or complete, he told of the kinfolk, of his commission to murder Kazi, and of his brief service with Janos. And he told of Ahmed, who also was a spy set to report on Janos through the psi tuner.

The old knight's eyes were bright with anger as he arose from his chair. "So this Ahmed looked into our minds when we had audiences with Janos and told him what we thought to keep secret. A lot of things are becoming clear to me now," he said grimly. "We'll have to overthrow him."

"I have not finished, m' Lord. The king has killed Ahmed with his own hand."

Miklos sat down again, confused and prepared to listen.

Nils told of his friendship with Imre Rakosi, of Kazi's demanding the boy, and of their going.

"And Janos sent him! The man is gutless!"

Nils went on to tell of Imre's murder. "But I was lucky enough to escape and returned to Pest to tell the king, and Janos cut Ahmed's throat. And Ahmed had a magic box he used to talk to his master's mind from afar. I know the use of such boxes, and used it to speak to my teacher who lives near the Northern Sea. He told me that Kazi has struck north against the Ukrainians. Casimir of Poland is gathering his army to join the Ukrainians, but he in turn has been invaded by barbarians from the north, so he can send only part of his army against Kazi."

Miklos was on his feet. "Why, man, *we* should go. Before we are alone. Throw down the traitor and go ourselves. There are no finer fighters in the world than Magyars. I . . ."

Nils interrupted. "That's what Janos plans to do. It's the reason he's called for his nobles. 'We must move for better or for worse,' he said, 'and if need be we'll die like men, with swords in our hands'"

Miklos stared. "Janos said that? *This* Janos?" His gaze sharpened. "Why did you come here to tell me this when I'll hear it from Janos himself in a few days? And why did you ask that your visit here be kept secret from him?"

The nobleman's mind was suddenly dark with suspicion.

"Because you've distrusted and despised Janos and might not believe him, while you might well believe me. And you'll be the key man among the nobles. For you are not only the most powerful of them; you're also the most respected, even by your enemies. If you respond with belief and approve the king's plan, the others will follow. But if Janos knew I'd taken it on myself to come here, he'd be mad. My forwardness has already tried his patience."

Miklos looked shrewdly at Nils. "I'll bet it has, at that. I look forward to seeing more of you, northman, for you're as crafty as you are strong, and I enjoy craft in an honest man."

"You'll be disappointed then, m' Lord, because I'm leaving tomorrow. The barbarians distracting Casimir are my own people, and I have to try to bring them in with us instead of unknowingly against us. If you see me again, it will be with them, the tribes of northmen, who, I have to tell you frankly, are the greatest fighters in the world."

It was then Miklos tested Nils. *You've said a lot today*, he thought silently but deliberately, *most of it hard to believe, and asked me to accept it as true. You've asked me to trust Janos, a man I've always distrusted with what I know now to be good reason. So tell me, can you really read my mind?*

The grin came back to Nils's face. "Yes m' Lord, and the honest doubts that go with the thoughts."

And Miklos smiled, the first smile Nils had seen on him. "That settles it. I'll do as you ask." He put out a big knobby hand that Nils wrapped in his.

"Thank you, m' Lord." Nils started to leave, then turned at the door. "And sir, don't underestimate the king. His mind does prefer the devious, just as you once told me, but he is no coward."

That evening Nils introduced Zoltan Kossuth to Janos, and the Bear showed no sign of surliness, for he was nothing if not shrewd. And they talked until late.

In the morning Nils rode north from the city astride a large strong horse, a prize of Magyar horse breeding. And with him rode Bela and a tough guard corporal also named Bela, differentiated by the guard as Bela One and Bela Two. Fourteen days later seventeen hundred Magyar knights left the fields outside Pest, with Janos and the western lords. By the time they reached the northeastern end of the kingdom and were ready to start over Uzhok Pass for the Ukraine, they had been joined by the eastern lords with twenty-one hundred more.

18.

A strip of wet meadow, roughly half a mile wide, bordered the brook. Several knights stood looking south into it, hands on sword hilts, watching three men ride toward them. One of the knights turned toward an awning stretched between young aspens and shouted in Polish. An officer ducked out from beneath the canopy, moving easily despite his heavy mail shirt, buckling on a sword. His helmet covered his ears and the back of his strong neck, and from the temples two steel eagle's wings projected.

The three men had approached near enough now to be recognized as a mixed lot. Two were knights, lanceless but wearing mail shirts and swords, their shields strapped behind one shoulder. The third was clearly one of the northern barbarians, a shirtless giant thickly muscled, with his blond hair in short braids, the skin of a wolf's head laced over his steel cap.

All three were well mounted, with a string of spares behind, and horses and men looked to have traveled a long way in a hurry.

The officer swung onto his mount. "Halt!" His command was in Polish, but the meaning was plain. "Identify yourselves!" That was not so clear but could be guessed.

Bela One spoke loudly in Anglic. "We are from the court of Janos III, King of the Magyars, who has gone with his army to fight the hordes of Baalzebub. We have come to see Casimir, King of the Poles."

The Pole scowled. "You have a northman with you."

"True. He has been in the service of Janos," Bela replied, "and has come to lead the northmen against Baalzebub. His name is Iron Hand, Järnhann in his language, and your king knows of him."

Nils spoke then, his voice casual but strong and easily heard. "You mistrust us. We'll give you our weapons if you want; we don't need them among friends. And send word to Jan Reszke that we've arrived."

The hard-eyed knight stared narrowly at them for a moment, then turned and shouted abruptly toward the awning. A younger officer emerged buckling his harness, and mounted the horse led him by a squire. Several other knights rode out of the woods, their faces curious or distrustful.

"Your weapons," the officer ordered in Anglic. The two Belas turned worriedly to Nils, but he was unbuckling his harness so they reluctantly surrendered theirs. The officer then led them through a belt of woods and into a trampled meadow that sloped gradually toward a marsh some five kilometers away. On the far side of the marsh, which seemed two or three kilometers across, Nils saw a long broken line of low dunes, dark with pine, where he supposed the northmen were.

A stream flowed out of the woods nearby and toward the distant marsh. On both sides of it were orderly ranks of colored tents and tethered horses covering scores of hectares. They rode among them and soon saw what they knew must be the tent of Casimir. Like the others, its canopy was brightly striped, and the sides were rolled up to let the air through. But its diameter was at least twenty meters; it was surrounded by a substantial open space, and the banner above it was larger and stood higher than any other. Their guide stopped them a short distance away and one of their escort rode ahead. Some knights came out of the king's tent and squinted suspiciously at them through the bright sunlight. Then one swung onto a saddled horse and rode the few score meters across to them. He stared truculently at Nils.

"Dismount!" he ordered loudly in Anglic. "And follow me." The three swung from their horses and started forward. "Just the northman," the knight snapped. "The other two swine stay here."

Nils strode over to him and looked up through slitted eyes. "Listen to me, knight, and listen carefully." His voice was soft but intense, and somehow it carried. "I've had too much hard mouth since I came here, and you'd better not give me any more. Either my friends come with me or I'm going to pull you off that horse and break your neck." He sensed the listening Poles.

The two men locked eyes, one an armed and mounted knight in linen shirt and spurred boots, the other a barefoot and unarmed youth on foot, his torso smeared with sweat and road dust. For a moment the knight's hand hovered above his sword hilt, but he did not grasp it. He looked back toward the king's tent; Casimir had emerged and was looking across, as if waiting for them. The knight swore in Polish and turned his horse. "Come then, all three," he said hoarsely, and they led their horses toward the king while the escort that had brought them looked at one another, impressed.

In his prime, Casimir had been a famous fighter. He was still a strong man, but so overgrown with fat that he had to be lifted onto his horse. But his brain was not fat, and the fiery recklessness of his youth had given way to an uncommonly logical pragmatism. He was not yet forty and, given a reasonable life span, might have ruled much more than Poland, had not Kazi come into the picture. He stood in a robe of bleached linen embroidered with gold thread, and a light golden circlet sat on his brown hair. One fat hand wearing a huge signet ring rested casually on the golden haft of a dagger, a sign of authority.

Jan Reszke, his chief counselor, contrasted sharply. A gangling stork of a man, his two meters of height made him one of the tallest men in Europe, but he weighed much less than Casimir.

As they neared the king, the knight barred their way with his drawn sword.

"Who are you and what do you want?" the king asked in Anglic, although he'd already been told.

"I am Nils Järnhann, warrior of the Svear, recently in service to King Janos of Hungary. My friends are from Janos' guard.

"I have visited the court of Baalzebub, fought in his arena, and seen his vileness. My greatest feat was escaping alive.

"I've been told that you're sending an army against Baalzebub and would send another except for the northmen landing on your shore.

"Word was to be sent to the tribes that I am coming. Baalzebub's land is broad and rich. I've come to lead the tribes against him, and when he's destroyed, we'll take his land." Nils folded his thick, sinewy arms across his chest and looked calmly at the king, his speech finished.

"And why should I believe you can do that?" Casimir asked.

"You're not damaged if I fail and a lot better off if I succeed."

"You mistake my meaning, barbarian," Casimir said, "or misuse it, more likely, if what I suspect of you is true. Never mind. Most likely you'll have a chance to prove yourself."

Nils shot a question to Jan Reszke. "Yes," Reszke thought back, "he knows—has known for years. He deduced psi without ever having heard of it, from listening to my council and considering the possible sources of my knowledge. Since then I've shown him the tuner."

Casimir glanced from one psi to the other, his narrow, full-lipped mouth amused in the gold-streaked brown beard, then spoke in Anglic. "Guard Master!" The surly knight stepped forward hopefully, sword still in his hand. "Jan Reszke and I will confer privately with the northman. I don't want to be disturbed unless there is an emergency. Meanwhile, see to the comfort of these two knights." Casimir gestured toward the Belas. "They have ridden hundreds of kilometers in haste, and I doubt they've had a proper meal in days. When they're refreshed, quarter them with my household knights.

And Stefan," he added, gesturing toward Nils with his head, "you have called the barbarians a pack of wolves. Don't curse the wolves 'til we see who they bite."

They entered the royal tent and Casimir lowered himself onto a cushioned seat, gesturing toward two seats facing his. "Sit there. I want to see your faces while we talk. I'll ask again the question that you didn't answer when I asked before. Why should I believe the northmen will follow you? And why should I believe they will fight Baalzebub if I let them out? And finally, why should I believe they can make a difference, as few as they are?"

Nils looked squarely back at him. "The tribes elect their leaders. Chiefs are chosen by all free men for their wisdom and justice. Raid leaders are chosen from among the warriors, by the warriors, for imagination and cunning. War chiefs are selected from among the raid leaders.

"Now the tribes are migrating, and I know something about the world they are entering—much more than almost any of them. They have no doubt selected a war chief already, but they'll listen carefully to anyone with experience here. Also, you have guessed what I am and know the advantage it gives me.

"And finally, I expect to go to them with your oath that you will let them pass untroubled if they in turn give their oath to join you against Baalzebub. And if they give it, they'll keep it. Besides that, I will tell them truthfully that if they don't fight him now with powerful allies, they will have to fight him later with little help and less hope.

"As for their value as allies—haven't some of

your people fought them? Why did you bring this
army here instead of a small force? When all the
warriors have landed, there should be two thousand of them or more. And if you chose ten of
them blindly, by lot, you couldn't match them
with your ten champions. Our freeholders will fight
too, if needed. They are skilled bowmen and familiar with swords.

"If you furnish them ships, they will surely ally
themselves with you, and they could be landed
faster and be ready to move sooner."

"All right," said Casimir. "You sound as if you
might pull it off at that. Jan has already made a
strong case for you, and if I didn't respect his
judgement, I wouldn't keep him around. Besides,
when things are bad enough, one does things he
might not do otherwise. As for ships, I've already
furnished some unwittingly, but I can send more.
I'll order them landed to take on guides from among
your people. But see to it that they are met peace-
fully and the crews well treated. If you fail me in
that, I will see you all dead. I'll send a messenger
now. When will you go to your northmen?"

"Let me ask a few questions, then feed me and I'll
go," Nils answered. "But let my two companions
stay with you, for among the tribes almost no one
knows Anglic. And among your people they'll find
customs much more like their own. They came with
me only to help discourage robbers along the way."

"Tadeus!" Casimir bellowed, and a page hurried
into the tent. "See that food is prepared for the
northman and me. And have a fast messenger sent
to me, prepared for a hard ride to Nowy Gdansk.
Go!" He turned to Nils as the boy hurried out.
"And when you talk to Jan, talk out loud."

*   *   *

"Jan," said Nils, "ask Raadgiver to have Danish ships sent to harbors in Jötmark and Norskland to help move the tribes. It may be hard to do, but we need to speed things as much as possible. And have you heard from the Magyars?"

"The western lords have left Pest. They are on their way."

"And what about the fighting?"

"We've lost contact with our man with the Ukrainians. He's probably dead. Yesterday we had a message by courier but it was a week old. Our army under Lord Bronislaw still had not come to any Ukrainian troops; apparently the fighting is well to the south yet."

"How large are the combined forces against Kazi?" Nils asked.

"The Ukrainians began with over six thousand and there will soon be another four thousand in action under Bronislaw, including nearly a thousand Saxons under the banner of Duke Hermann. The Magyars will add thirty-eight hundred or so. We have three thousand here and Albert of Prussia is holding fifteen hundred against the northmen, all of which can be sent when we have an agreement with your people." He paused. "And later, of course, your two thousand northmen." The latter had been hard for him to say; it still was not real to him that Nils could settle this confrontation of Poles and neovikings and bring his people in. "Some of the independent west German nobles are raising their armies too," he went on, "but it's hard to know how many they'll come to or when they'll start."

Casimir interrupted. "You've been in Baalzebub's

land. What do you know about his army? How big is it, and how good?"

Nils looked at him squarely while answering. "It numbers about thirty thousand and it's supposed to be very good. Twenty thousand are horse barbarians, eastern tribes that have allied themselves with him. The other ten thousand are his personal army, men he calls orcs, who are proud of their brutality. I expect the horse barbarians are very dangerous in the open, but it may be they won't fight as skillfully in timber, especially if they have to get off their horses. The orcs are probably as good on foot as on horseback. Some of the orc officers are psis; they'll be hard to ambush, and if they have tuners, they'll be able to coordinate their units better in battle."

Casimir pursed his lips and scowled. "The odds sound more rotten all the time. Maybe it would be better to surrender."

"Kazi—Baalzebub, that is—wants to conquer and rule for just one reason. He loves to debase and destroy. Public tortures are his entertainment and the entertainment of his orcs. You'd be far better off to die in the saddle than in the arena, and in the meantime there will be the game of war to enjoy."

Casimir grunted.

"His strengths are obvious, but he has weaknesses, too," Nils went on. "At one time he must have been a thinker and planner, but now he doesn't seem able to hold one matter in his mind and concentrate. And he acts foolishly. One of his whims turned the King of Hungary from a reluctant ally into a total enemy. So we are four thousand stronger and he's four thousand weaker.

"I won't try to mislead you, though. With his power he can make mistakes and still win. But there is a chance, and it's the northmen that make that chance real."

Casimir looked glumly at nothing while Nils turned his eyes to Jan Reszke. "Has Raadgiver had a man among the tribes?"

"Yes, and he's reported to me. He spread the word among them that the Yngling was coming from the south to lead them to a land of rich grass and fat cattle. He's a master wordsmith. They called a council and listened to him. Now they're waiting to see what happens."

"I'll go and eat," Nils said. "And I'll want to take three squires to use as messengers."

Nils walked rapidly through the marsh, his bare feet automatically finding the firm places where there were any and slopping nonchalantly in the water or ooze where there were not. Three young Poles hurried behind, apprehensive, muddy, and unhappy.

Nils's eyes searched the forest edge ahead. Their approach was open and it was certain they'd been seen. He had spotted brief movement once and could sense watchfulness; now he began to pick up the quiet thoughts of men speaking.

"It's one of ours. Do you know him?"

"No. From here he looks big; if I knew him, I'd recognize him. What are those outlanders with him? He doesn't seem to hold them prisoner. Knut, go and get Leif Trollsverd; there's something strange about this."

"My blood. He *is* a big one. If he was to wrestle a bear, I'd bet againat the bear."

The edge of the marsh was a ribbon of slough into which a pine had fallen from the forest margin. Nils sprang to it and picked his way through its branches toward the dry ground. The tallest of the squires sprang too, missing with a splash. The other two simply waded glumly in.

"Halt!"

The squires stopped abruptly in surprise, standing almost to their crotches in the dark water. The forest was fringed with alder shrubs, and they hadn't seen the two warriors who now stepped out to the water's edge.

"What have you got there?" The speaker's blond beard hung in two short braids, and over his steel cap was the headskin of a bull seal. Both the totem and the accent were unfamiliar to Nils and he supposed they were Norskar.

"They are messengers loaned to me by Casimir, the Polish king."

The warrior's brows raised. The Polish king? That would be their chief, he thought. "Well, tell your messengers to get out of the mire before they sink out of sight," he said. "We were posted here as sentries, and while three Polish sprouts in the keeping of a warrior hardly amounts to an attack, you'd better wait here a bit anyhow. I've sent for our group leader."

Nils and the young Poles walked into the woods with the sentries and sat on the ground. Within a minute two more warriors of the Seal Clan trotted down through the pines, and Nils arose. Leif Trollsverd was rather small for a warrior, a young man whose thin skin and sharply defined muscu-

larity gave him a startlingly sinewy and aggres-
sive appearance. His dark complexion and black
hair looked more Mediterranean than Scandinavian.

"Have you got prisoners there?" he asked Nils;
even his words were quick.

"No. They are messengers loaned to me by
Casimir, the Polish king."

"And who are you? I've never seen you before."

"I am Nils Järnhann of the Svear, and I've never
been here before. I've come here from a kingdom
far to the south, the land of the Magyars, to speak
to the war council."

The group leader looked Nils over from head to
foot, his sharp eyes absorbing a score of details.
"From the south. Come then. I'll take you to Björn
Ärrbuk, our war leader. He is of your tribe." Leif
Trollsverd turned and loped off, followed by Nils
and the discouraged-looking squires.

The seaward dunes too had long since stabilized
here and were forested, and the camp of Björn
Ärrbuk was on one of them. The war leader stood
with his runners on the beach, watching a captured Polish ship work its way around a sandspit
offshore.

He turned as they approached. "Ha, what are
these?" he asked, looking at the young Poles.

"They came from the Polish camp. With him,"
Trollsverd said, indicating Nils with his thumb.
"He is Nils Järnhann of your tribe, who has come
here from the south and wants to meet with the
war council." The Norwegian looked meaningfully
at Ärrbuk, then turned and trotted away into the
woods.

Björn Ärrbuk was of middle height and middle
age, his barrel chest, short, thick legs and long

arms giving him an apelike look. Even his hair was an orangutan red. A scar crossed his abdomen diagonally from the lower left to the rib cage, providing his surname. A physician of eight hundred years before might have wondered how he survived such a cut without twenty-first century technology, or surviving, how he could have become fit again. But he was fit and enormously strong, with the vitality of the bear that was his totem and his life name, and given to impulsive wrestling with any warrior at hand.

He glanced sideways at Nils. "I've seen you somewhere," he said, and turned to watch the ship again. Its sail was furled against an offshore wind, and strong arms pulled the oars. "It's from Svealann," said the war leader. "Of the three tribes, six hundred warriors have landed. But the only way we'll get all the people ashore before winter is to steal more ships, and that's costly business. They're heavily guarded at the docks now, and flee from us at sea."

"The King of Poland is sending us ships," Nils replied. "They'll land here in a few days for guides to take them to the tribes so we can land people faster. And it may be that Jørgen Stennaeve of the Danes will also send ships, to Norskland and Jötmark."

Björn Ärrbuk turned and stared at the tall warrior beside him. "The King of the Poles? You must be crazy. The King of the Poles has brought an army to try to wïpe us out when we leave this place."

"I'm not crazy," Nils answered calmly. "I've just talked with him and he gave his oath. But it's not a simple story and he wants something in return. I came to tell it to the war council, but if you want me to, I'll tell it to you now and again to them later."

The burly chief stepped back from him, perplexed and a little irritated, his body half crouched in unconscious response. "What's your name again?" he asked at length, straightening.

"Nils Järnhann. You were at the ting a year ago when I was banished. When I was a sword apprentice, I struck a warrior and killed him. A great deal has happened to me in that year. I've traveled far and learned a lot."

"I remember. Yes. Some of the Eagle Clan believed we should have decorated a pole with your head and that Axel Stornäve favored you because you were of his clan." Ärrbuk chuckled. "Actually Kalle Blåtann was a bully and braggart, and even in his own clan there were those who thought he had gotten what was overdue to him. Had the law allowed, we might have let you off free." He turned serious then. "What you say about the Polish king is hard to believe, but we have heard things about you. I'll call the council—all that have landed. Isbjørn Hjeltesøn is here, and the chiefs of several clans as well as group leaders. I'll gather them for the evening meal. But now I want to see who lands with this ship."

Seventy warriors of the Reindeer Clan landed— all that clan had, for it was the smallest of the Svear. Then the ship sculled out past the sandspit, powered by the strong arms of Sea Eagle clansmen. It's sail was hoisted into the offshore wind and it started north for the Glutton fishing village of Jäävham.

Björn showed Nils the council circle, then trotted off with his runners to find the members of the war council while Nils gathered twigs and piled them carefully among the ashes and char of the fire site.

19.

The long double file of neovikings was not very impressive as they rode down the dusty road. They numbered twenty-two hundred warriors and four hundred freeholders—filthy, shirtless, and riding bareback on nondescript workhorses that Casimir's officers had commandeered from the farms of north-western Poland. Now they were entering the northern Ukraine. Kazi's army had advanced far during the summer, and the northmen moved with scouts ahead and on both flanks. One of the lead scouts galloped back into sight and fell in beside Björn Ärrbuk and Nils.

"We've run into some knights," he reported laconically. "Our Pole thinks they're Magyars because he can't understand anything they say."

The few northmen besides Nils and Sten Vannaren who knew appreciable Anglic had been assigned to scout groups. And Casimir had early assigned several knights—men who knew some Danish—to the neoviking army to serve as contacts and interpreters.

Nils and Björn dug bare heels into their horses'

sides and galloped heavily up the road. In less than two kilometers they caught the lead scouts, with their Pole and five Magyar knights. The Magyars were in bad shape, three of them bandaged and all five tired and demoralized. They were remnants of a group that had ambushed a large force of horse barbarians. Badly outnumbered to begin with, they had planned to strike and then ride to cover in the forest, leaving part of their number among the trees as archers to give them cover when they disengaged. This had been more or less effective before. But the horse barbarians had been bait, and when the Magyars had ridden out in attack, their archers had been surprised from behind by a company of orcs. The whole party had been caught between the two enemy forces.

"There were three hundred of us, nearly," their officer added, "and as far as I know, we're all that's left." The man stopped talking for a few seconds, his haggard face working. "And I doubt we killed fifty in the fight."

Nils sensed that these men no longer had hope of victory or even survival; they hoped only to sell their lives dearly. This time they had failed even that.

"You're the first Magyars we've come to," Nils said. "How many of you are left?"

"I don't know. I only know our losses have been heavy. But we don't operate as an army. At the beginning we separated into ten squadrons of three to five hundred each. We've done some regrouping since, as chance allowed, to bring the strength of the squadrons back up to that. Probably more than half of us lie dead, and Janos one of them."

"What of the other armies—the Ukrainians and Poles and Germans?"

"I've seen them several times but never talked to any. I speak no Anglic. But those who do say they've lost heavily, too, especially the Ukrainians, who were in it from the beginning." The man stopped again, looking like he might have cried had there been any tears in him. "We've probably lost more than the enemy, and we were a lot fewer to begin with.

"But I'll tell you this. After what I've seen, if I could get out of this safe, I wouldn't do it. I want to die with my teeth in a throat."

At midday, when the column stopped to water and rest their horses, a grim Magyar was assigned to each scouting group. That night they camped in a forest and stayed there the next day while scouts on their best horses searched the country ahead, where large prairies were interspersed with forests and woods. In the late afternoon they returned to report a large encampment of horse barbarians.

Björn Ärrbuk gathered several groups, a total of three hundred warriors, and rode quietly out in the gathering dusk. After a time they saw enemy fires in the distance; clearly the enemy was not afraid of attack. Hooding their horses they lay down to rest.

Gradually the distant fires burned down and most of the warriors slipped out into the prairie on foot, disappearing into the darkness. The men who stayed behind with the horses watched and listened intently. Once they heard a mounted patrol pass at some distance in the darkness, and then it was quiet again.

Suddenly there were distant brassy blasts from foreign war horns, and fires blazed up. They pulled the hoods from their own mounts and sprang onto their bare backs, ready, nervous to know what was happening. In a few minutes they could hear the thunder of approaching hooves, the hooting of neoviking war horns, and then shouts in their own language. A herd of horses galloped past, driven by whooping northmen, and they rode in among them individually, changing mounts in the tumult.

When morning came to the neoviking camp, the group leaders counted their men. All but twenty-one had returned, straggling in on fine horses and driving others, blood on their swords and grins on their faces. They could not say how many they'd killed, but they thought a hundred at least, and they'd scattered a large part of the horses that they had not been able to steal. Once mounted, they had cut a spiral swath through the enemy camp before fleeing, and they all agreed it had been worth the long trip from the homeland.

Björn Ärrbuk sent out two of his Poles and two Magyars to hunt for others of their own forces and spread word of the victory. Meanwhile scouts were dispatched again, much better mounted now, if still bareback, to get a better understanding of the country and the location of enemy camps. Groups not chosen for the first raid were impatient for action.

Another large encampment of horse barbarians was reported about twenty kilometers away. A few kilometers from it was a dense wood of several score hectares, forming a small island in the prairie. Björn Ärrbuk called a council.

"Nils Järnhann tells me we may be able to surprise horse barbarians but never the orcs, because the orcs have mind readers like himself who could sense our coming. If we want to kill orcs, the best thing is to have them come to us at a place of our own choosing. If we surprise the barbarian camp in the dark and then take cover in the woods nearby, they can surround us. They can attack us there if they want, but their horses will only be a hindrance to them in the timber and we can butcher to our hearts' content. Nils thinks they will send for orcs, though, to root us out on foot, and we can find out just what these orcs are made of.

"There's a spring in the woods for water, and it's less than three kilometers from a large stretch of forest, so that we can sneak out and escape by night when we want to.

"We'll be both bait and trap, and when we're done they'll have learned to hate and fear the northmen."

They broke camp at sundown and rode by moonlight to the woods near the enemy camp without encountering a patrol, then lay down to sleep until the moon set.

This time the raiders moved out on horseback, four hundred of them, silent until a patrol challenged them less than five hundred meters from the enemy camp. With loud whoops they charged, striking at anyone on foot as horse barbarians ran among the tents. Through the camp and back again they rode, chopping and striking in the confusion and darkness, then broke up and rode away hard into the concealment of night. Their shouts and laughter as they straggled into their own camp might have kept everyone awake until dawn if the group leaders hadn't insisted that they quiet down and rest.

Soon after daybreak several thousand horse barbarians were circling the woods and looking grimly into its thickets while more arrived periodically from other camps. Several times impatient groups charged their horses toward the woods, breaking off when swarms of arrows met them near the trees from freeholders stationed among the branches and from warriors on the ground.

About midday a large army of mounted men wearing black mail came into sight in broad, ordered columns, dismounting out of bow shot. Men in the treetops counted the width of the columns and the number of ranks and shouted down that there were about four thousand. The freeholders were ordered out of the trees. The orcs formed a line of battle, several deep, opposite one side of the woods and then, shields raised, began to walk forward. At thirty meters a war horn blew from among the trees, triggering a flight of arrows, and the orcs began to double time toward the woods.

Once engaged, the warriors drew back, tightening their protective line around the freeholders and the horse herd. The battle continued until midafternoon between the mailed and grimly silent orcs and the shouting, grinning northmen, and as the hours passed, the orcs became grimmer. Finally trumpets sounded and they began an orderly retreat. The northmen permitted them to disengage and followed them with twanging bows until they were out of range in the prairie.

For the rest of the day the neovikings moved among the trees, taking scalps, equipping themselves with black mail shirts, and dragging orc bodies to the edge of the prairie where they piled the mutilated corpses for the enlightenment of the watching horse barbarians, shouting their counts to the tallymen and exchanging clouts of exuberance. The scalps numbered seventeen hundred and thirty-seven. Their own dead came to a hundred and ninety-six, and they released sixty-five more whose bodies were too badly wounded to ride.

"So those are the orcs." Björn Ärrbuk laughed. "You told me they are the toughest we'll see on the ground. Surely that can't be true."

Nils nodded. "It's too bad they broke off when they did; they were getting tired faster than we were. And we may have trouble getting them to fight us again on ground of our own choosing."

Björn turned to his runners. "Make sure that enough sentries are out and have the men eat and get some sleep. We'd better get out of here tonight. When the moon sets we'll sneak across to the big body of timber where we can move around again."

The next day the northmen camped in the forest. Their nighttime crossing hadn't gone undetected for long, but they had maintained stealth even among the questing squadrons of horse barbarians, moving through the blackness in small groups or singly, breaking into a gallop and fighting only when they had to. Many abandoned their horses for diversion and slunk across on foot. They scattered everywhere, reassembling in the forest with the locational sense of the wilderness-bred. At daybreak they counted ninety-seven missing and were in a vile mood.

The day was spent napping and filing the nicks

out of their swords while small mounted patrols went out to explore the forest. One patrol found a band of fewer than thirty Poles and Ukrainians, all that were left of a mixed force of three hundred who had fought a pitched battle with a large force of orcs two days earlier. Another patrol watched an attack on horse barbarians by a large number of Magyars, who seemed to have abandoned their small-unit tactics for hit-and-run attacks by larger forces. The battle was brief and bloody, and about eight hundred effectives reached the cover of the trees where, after brief fighting, the horse barbarians had broken off the engagement.

Men of the patrol led Nils to the Magyars. They had reassembled deep in the forest and were camped by a brook, sharpening their weapons and nursing their wounds. Nils recognized their commander and the burly psi who squatted beside him, eating their horsemeat in the shade of a linden.

"Lord Miklos!" Nils called. "Zoltan!"

The tall knight got up slowly. "Nils. So we do meet again." He spoke and thought like a man half-asleep. "We heard that the northmen had come and that they'd even night-raided the very camps of the enemy. Butchering him and running off his horses. You can't be as good as we've heard, but we enjoyed the stories." He sounded apathetic, as if he had not actually enjoyed anything for a long while. "Did you know that Janos is dead? In our first battle."

Tears welled in the dull eyes. "I'm all used up, friend; I didn't realize how old I'd become. But I won't need to last much longer. As far as I know, the eight hundred you find of us here are all that are left of thirty-eight hundred that crossed Uzhok

Pass. We've done our best, but we've been out-numbered time and again, and our spirits are dying with our friends. We have no hope. Even our hate is dulled; the fire is dead in it."

"If you'd been with us yesterday, it might have been relit," Nils said quietly. "We got four thousand orcs to attack us in heavy timber, and when they pulled out, they left more than seventeen hundred dead. We took scalps enough to have made a large tent, and our own losses were two hundred sixty."

The gray Magyar looked up at Nils for the first time. "How many of you are there?"

"We started with twenty-two hundred warriors and have lost four hundred, while seventy more have wounds bad enough to impair their fighting. We released the spirits of those who were badly wounded. We couldn't take them with us and wouldn't leave them for the enemy."

Miklos nodded. "We, too. We've seen what they do to their prisoners. What will you do next?"

"We're exploring, patrolling, so we can decide what's to our advantage. We always look for an advantage. Come with me and meet our war leader, Björn Ärrbuk. You can help us plan." The invitation was a gesture; he knew, approximately, what the answer would be.

"How old are you, big friend?"

"This is my twentieth summer."

The old knight shook his head. "Perhaps tomorrow, if I can. If nothing happens. But today I must rest."

By evening another patrol reported two small forces of Poles and Ukrainians in the forest, totalling two hundred and eighty effectives. The various reports also gave a picture of the tactical situation. This forest too was almost an island in the prairie, but a big one, about twenty kilometers long and mostly five to eight wide. It connected with more extensive forests to the west by a neck of timber about a kilometer wide. Strong forces of horse barbarians patrolled the prairie on both sides and an army of orcs were digging a ditch and piling a barricade of felled trees across the neck.

Björn Ärrbuk called his officers together. "Have the men break camp. We're going to move out right now so we can travel while the moon is still up. We'll camp about a kilometer from the orc line. Nils, go to your friend, the Magyar chief, and to the others, the Poles and Ukrainians. Tell them we are all surrounded and we're going to break out at sunup. Tell them we want their help, but we won't wait for it. If they won't come now, we'll leave them to fry in their own grease. Meet us at our new camp." The war leader grinned and punched Nils's shoulder. "Tell them we're going to kill lots of orcs tomorrow and they can watch."

With dawn came the first freeze, crisping the grass. The Slavic and Magyar cavalry, along with neoviking freeholders and wounded, were in flanking positions as the light grew, ready with bows to repel any horse barbarians who might try to enter the woods and intervene. Orc psis had picked up the approach of the warriors in the growing light, and they were ready.

Initially the northmen, attacking up the ditch bank and across the barricade, took heavy losses. But they broke the orc line in places and soon pushed it back. Some of the orcs were clearly afraid of the northmen, but their ranks were deep and their officers ruthlessly permitted no withdrawal. The battle continued without slowing until mid-morning, when the orcs began to unravel from exhaustion and their casualties began to increase rapidly. Then, without warning, hundreds of fresh orcs counterattacked, keeping up a relentless pressure for half an hour. Suddenly orc trumpets sounded and their survivors withdrew with a semblance of order.

The northmen did not pursue them. Instead, they pulled off the mail shirts they weren't yet accustomed to and sprawled in the shade or wandered limply around, foul with sweat, hands cramped, their hoots and crowing almost giddy with fatigue. Gradually their group leaders got them organized again, got outposts manned, and the scalping began. Some of the knights came, their faces shifting out of dullness as they watched. A few wept quietly, bitterly, as if reawakening into awareness and grief. Others turned grim and straight-mouthed and went away. As the number of scalps grew, the barbarian vitality began to reassert itself, with counts shouted back and forth from squad to squad. More knights came on horseback now, to drop loops around the necks of scalped orcs, dragging the bodies into big piles. And soon almost every northman, even Nils, had a mail shirt that fitted.

The final count almost equalled that of the earlier battle—fifteen hundred and sixty-eight. But the northmen killed by the orcs or dispatched by their comrades numbered four hundred and eighty-nine, chief among them being Björn Ärrbuk. After the tally the war council met to choose a new war leader, and a group leader of the Jötar arose.

"In both battles my group has fought next to a group of the Norskar whose leader is called Leif Trollsverd. I was too busy to watch others much, and anywhere I looked I saw great sword work. But I can tell you why he is called Trollsverd; his blade seemed truly enchanted. If we had an army of Trollsverds, there'd be no orcs left at all. I say we should make him our new war leader."

Leif Trollsverd got up, bloody and filthy, looking around the council, and his words were not as fast as usual. "I have always known I was good," he said. "I could see it for myself and I've always been praised for it. But until this week I never realized how good I had to be to stand out among the rest—not until I saw how much better they were than these orc swine who are supposed to be the best of any other army.

"But also I've always known that there are others around me who are much more clever than I. I have never led a major raid, for there have always been others who could see possibilities better and plan more cleverly. They are better fitted than I to be war chief, even though my sword may kill more orcs.

"Look around. Who is the most knowing among us? Who was it Björn Ärrbuk questioned about the enemy before deciding his moves?

"The Danish poem-smith said The Yngling would appear among us, and I think he was right. And many others believe the same. I say we should make Nils Järnhann war chief."

* * *

That night the living northmen slept almost as soundly as their dead. But before their new war leader slept, he went to visit the Magyars and Slavs. He sensed the turgidity of feeling among them. They were alive again. They had seen great killing of a hated enemy that day and their emotions were stretched with a desire to do the same.

In the morning several thousand horse barbarians approached to within a kilometer of the timber's edge. Without council or command, a group of Magyar knights galloped out toward them, and within moments the whole force of Magyar and Slavic cavalry poured after, spontaneously, almost helter-skelter, forming a loose line of attack as they charged. The horse barbarians formed to meet them, shouting war cries, but the knights penetrated them deeply, fighting like berserkers.

The northmen, those still with horses, mounted and watched from the timber's edge. They had neither lances nor saddles, nor were they the horsemen the others were, so Nils commanded them to stand unless he signaled.

The battle broke into clusters of knights and horse barbarians wheeling and chopping, the savagery of the knights submerging groups of the enemy time and again, until a large number of horse barbarians disengaged, regrouped and charged. That wave broke, but it took good men with it, and the surviving knights at last gave way, riding for the timber while a rearguard stood for brief moments. Then the horse barbarians raced eagerly after them.

Looking around him, Nils raised his war horn. When the enemy was near enough, his people would loose their arrows, and any horse barbarians who attempted pursuit into the forest would die. But in that moment a new force appeared out of the timber's edge nearby, Polish and Prussian cavalry under the banner of Casimir. Without warning they launched themselves at the horse barbarians, who were strung out loosely in pursuit, and swept them away. Their horses were fresher, and they rode after the now-fleeing barbarians with a blood lust that had never been properly satisfied before.

For the rest of the morning, while the northmen helped themselves to horses, saddles and lances and refilled their quivers with arrows of Asian pattern, the allied cavalry enjoyed the grim satisfaction of counting enemy dead and killing enemy wounded. The count was more than twenty-one hundred. Perhaps the horse barbarians could afford twenty-one hundred more easily than the allies could afford the six hundred and eighty knights they had lost, but as Trollsverd remarked to Nils, the battle had changed their friends. They were a force to contend with now.

Lord Miklos had said he would not last much longer, and he had been right. The gaunt old warrior was found with a broken sword in his hand and his helmet split.

That afternoon, camped deep in a forest and with patrols out, the allied commanders met in council.

Of the nearly forty-five hundred Polish and Prussian knights that had ridden east with Casimir about two thousand effectives remained. Of the Magyars and Slavs who had launched the battle that morning, fewer than three hundred were still able to fight. The neovikings numbered thirteen hundred warriors fit for combat and nearly four hundred freeholders. Not counting the freeholders, the allied armies totalled less than thirty-seven hundred.

They estimated that Kazi's army, on the other hand, still must number twelve to fourteen thousand horse barbarians and more than six thousand orcs.

Zoltan Kossuth and Jan Reszke had been in contact with members of the Inner Circle and reported on other armies. The Danes and Frisians together had already started out with seventeen hundred knights, while an army of Austrians and Bavarians believed to number as many as two thousand had left or was about to leave. The lords of Provence, on the other hand, were still fighting one another. Casimir remarked wryly that they would be doing that until doomsday, which might be nearer than they appreciated. The French king had refused to commit himself until his exasperated nobles finally killed him. As soon as they could agree on a new king, which might take some time and fighting, they could provide an army of as many as five thousand.

When the two psis had finished their report, Casimir stood up and looked around. He had lost a lot of weight and a lot of men. "Who wants to bet that Kazi's army won't cross the French border before the French do?" he asked. "The fact is that those western cretins, the whole obscene bunch, sat around sucking their thumbs while we've been fighting. So we're still on our own, what there are left of us, while they squawk and flap their arms, and I guess we all know what that means."

Nils stood and answered the Polish king quietly. "You knew from the start that Kazi's strength was much greater than ours. But you chose to fight because the only other thing to do was worse. It still is. Now we can hurt Kazi most by killing more orcs. Without a strong army of orcs he'll lose his power over the chiefs of the horse tribes. But we can't get anything done by sitting here in the woods waiting to be attacked or letting him ride past us into the west. Tomorrow we need to send out a number of small patrols to learn where the enemy is camped and what he is doing."

"And then what?" Casimir challenged. "What will we do then?"

"We'll know when they come back. But it will be . . . as much as you could wish."

"Do not underestimate what I can wish, Northman."

Nils laughed, not derisively nor tactically but in open pleasure and admiration, startling the knights. "Let me correct my words," he said. "We will do as much, at least, as you might hope for."

"And how do you divine this?"

"I don't divine and I cannot say how, but it will happen."

By the following evening the patrols were returning. Several had found newly abandoned enemy campsites while two reported a huge new camp. Bunches of cattle were being driven there, and the fumes of many fires suggested that meat was being smoked.

"It sounds to me," Casimir said gruffly, "as if

Kazi has gathered his whole army together to pass us by and move west. Apparently we're too few to trouble with any longer." He looked at Nils. "What do we do now, Northman?"

A sentry hurried into the circle of firelight. "M' Lords," he broke in. "A patrol has brought a prisoner."

"When did we start taking prisoners?" Casimir growled.

"Not an enemy prisoner, Your Highness. It's a foreigner. There are a lot of them, sir—men, women and children—and this patrol ran into some of their scouts. The one they brought in speaks Anglic and offered to go with the patrol so that we wouldn't attack his people."

"Attack his people? We've got too many enemies already. What kind of people are they?"

"The one the patrol brought in says they're Finns, Your Highness, whatever Finns are, and that the whole race of them left their homeland in the north."

"Bring him here," Nils ordered. "I know a little about Finns. Maybe there'll be some help for us here."

The man was Kuusta Suomalainen; Nils sensed his idenity and also his psi before he could see him. The man had been trained.

The Finns totalled nine thousand, including nearly two thousand fighting men, but none were knights or warriors in the neoviking sense. They were roughly equivalent to the neoviking free-holders—independent, vigorous and tough, but with modest weapons skills except for excellent marksmanship. With a few others, Kuusta had been scouting a day ahead of the main body of migrants and saw the end of the battle between the knights and the horse barbarians. They had returned to their people then, and their headmen had elected to continue into the war zone, taking their chances on getting through safely.

"There is no safety," Nils told him. "Not anywhere in Europe while Kazi is alive. He has perhaps twenty thousand men while we have about four thousand. Sit and listen awhile, old friend. Maybe before the council is over, you'll offer your help."

The others deferring to him, Nils questioned the patrol leaders carefully. The Kazi camp was near the west bank of a river, in a long stretch of prairie some four to six kilometers wide that extended from great marshes on the north southward along the river for tens of kilometers. On the east side of the river, and protected by it from prairie fires, stood a forest.

Local knights knew the place. The river, although sixty or eighty meters wide, could be easily crossed at this season, when water levels were low and currents weak. But the steep banks were troublesome.

When no one else had any more information, Nils outlined his plan. There were more unknowns in the situation than any leader would like, but there was no time to scout the site himself. "This is our chance," he said. "We don't know how long they'll stay there, and if we miss it, we're not likely to get another as good. Tomorrow we'll rest and tomorrow night we'll ride." He turned to Casimir. "And don't feel left out, good friend. You'll have other chances, and the firesetters will be yours. But this action takes stealth and foot soldiers, so it has to be ours."

The next day Kuusta Suomalainen arrived with four hundred volunteers, brown-faced and sinewy, their quivers stuffed with arrows. The rest of the Finns would wait for the survivors to return.

The waxing moon gave good light until nearly dawn. Crouching quietly in the forest some distance from the river bank, the northmen tested the air for a breeze. Too many things could go wrong. At least there did not seem to be an east wind, although down among the trees a light breeze might go undetected. But they could smell the enemy horses across the river to the west. And while the clear night had lowered the temperature almost enough for another freeze, the air was dry enough that, even in the open, there was likely to be little dew on the grass.

Nils had slipped ahead and lay in the brush at the top of the riverbank, two meters above the water. Psi sentries would not detect his single quiet mind. In the dim light of dawn he could see thousands of horses in a great paddock that lay between the far bank and the enemy tents.

Finally the sun rose, brightening the kilometers of tall tawny grass beyond the enemy camp. Orcs and barbarians began to stir among the horses. A breeze came up, a good west breeze, and Nils could smell the horses strongly.

Back in the forest, men lay with the patience of those who hunt for their living.

Foreign thoughts mumbled faintly at the fringes of his awareness, a psionic background to the morning. As the sun slowly climbed, the breeze became brisk, and then he saw several lines of smoke across the prairie. They grew as he watched, coalescing.

He wiggled backward through the brush, got up, and slipped back to his men. The order passed down the line in both directions, in soft Scandinavian and by gestures to the Finns. Quietly, then, they moved toward the river, the freeholders and Finns selecting suitable trees along the bank.

Through the screen of vegetation they could see and hear some of the growing excitement in the enemy camp. Trumpets blew and men hurried about. The smoke of the distant prairie fire had grown to a tall curtain. Northmen and Finns reached back over their shoulders to make sure their arrows were within ready reach and came easily from the quiver. Barbarians and orcs began to trot into the horse park carrying saddles and gear, while others caught and soothed nervous horses. The freeholders and Finns started up their chosen trees with helpful boosts, keeping behind the trunks. Within a few moments a unit of orcs had mounted and were moving down the bank into the water. When they were two-thirds across, a war horn blew.

For half an hour arrows hissed into the ranks of soldiers. At first there were both orcs and horse barbarians in roughly similar numbers. Some made it across piecemeal, to die fighting at the top of a bank that grew slippery with splashings of water and blood. After a bit the horse barbarians stopped coming and could be seen riding along the bank in both directions, trying to outflank the long wall of flame accelerating toward them. But the disciplined mail-clad orcs kept coming. Many took arrows and disappeared. Some drowned in the deeper water when their horses were killed under them. Many scrambled out on foot, slipping and swearing, to face the deadly blades above them, or spurred dripping, falling horses up the bank. One by one they established bridgeheads and fought to expand them. Freeholders and Finns began to jump from the trees, quivers empty, running back through the forest to the place where the horses were tied. A war horn signalled that the enemy was crossing in force below the south flank of the neoviking line, and the warriors too began to run for their horses, shouting and crowing.

They galloped away almost unmolested, then slowed, jogging their horses northward through the forest until they approached the marsh. Scouts sent down to the river reported large numbers of horse barbarians on the opposite side who had outflanked the fire, perhaps by swimming their horses down the river. Nils had his men abandon their horses, and they moved into the marsh, hidden in the wilderness of tall reeds and cattails and safe from any cavalry attack.

Not far downstream they found a ford, crossed the broad, sluggish current, and started westward. They moved concealed well within the marsh's edge. It wouldn't do to be detected. If they were, there'd be no chance of reaching the remounts they'd left the night before.

"What do we do if someone's found the horses?" asked a blood-spattered warrior.

Nils grinned at him. "You're spoiled by all the riding we've done in this country. Imagine you're back in Svealann and be ready to walk. We'll know in a few kilometers."

After a bit a scout came through the reeds to him. "Nils," he said in an undertone. "We can see the woods where we left the horses. It's crawling with enemy."

Nils turned to his runners. "Hold the men up. I'm going to see what possibility there is of drawing them into a fight. I don't think they're foolish enough to attack us in the marsh, but we don't want to miss any chances."

He moved to the marsh's edge and lay on his belly in the muck, looking through a screen of reeds across the narrow band of prairie separating him from the woods. There were hundreds of mounted orcs in the vicinity; it would be suicide to try to reach the horses. Then he recognized a banner and his eyes narrowed. They were the elite guard.

Nils called out strong and clear in thought. "KAZI! (He projected an image of himself, sword bloody, foot on a dead orc.) HOW MANY MEN DID YOU LOSE TODAY? THREE THOUSAND? MORE! AND I DOUBT WE LOST MORE THAN A HUNDRED."

There was a commotion among the orcs as several psi officers caught the taunt, and a huge figure in glistening black mail rode out from the trees on a magnificent horse. Although Nils lay concealed, the face looked exactly at him.

"So it's you, Northman." The thought entered Nils's mind, cold and quiet. "Have you come to die?"

"Not me. We're enjoying ourselves too much."

Kazi's utter calm alerted him for some deadly surprise. "You like to watch butchery, Kazi. Why don't you send your orcs into the marsh?"

The great cold mind fixed on his without discernible thought or emotion, only deadly presence. Finally it spoke. "Will you fight me, Northman?"

"What assurance can you give that your men won't attack me if I come out?"

"I'll come most of the way to the marsh's edge," Kazi answered. "We'll be closer to your men than mine."

Again their minds locked for a moment, like eyes, and Nils read no sense of treachery there. Only grimness. He turned to his scouts. "The black giant is Kazi, the one called Baalzebub. We've spoken through the mind and agreed to fight, the two of us. If any of his people ride out toward us, blow a war horn and cover me so I'll have a chance to run for it."

Then he looked out through the fringe of reeds again while a line of archers formed behind him. Kazi was speaking to the officers with him in what seemed to be Arabic. Some of them rode in among the troops, but still Nils sensed no treachery.

After a moment Kazi dismounted and walked toward the marsh, slowly, his iron mind locked shut. When he had covered somewhat more than half the distance, he paused, and Nils came out of the reeds. They walked toward one another. To the northmen peering out, Kazi looked immense, emitting an aura of utter and indomitable force. When only a few meters separated them, they raised swords and shields, and then they met.

Kazi's first stroke would have severed a pine ten centimeters thick, but it was easily dodged, so that his sword nearly struck the ground and he barely caught Nils's counter on his shield. Shock flashed through Nils's mind: the man knew little of sword work. Kazi's second stroke followed too quickly after a feint, so that it lacked force and left him extended. Nils's shield deflected it easily and he struck Kazi's thigh, cleaving flesh and bone, knocked the black shield aside as Kazi fell, and sent his sword point through mail and abdomen, feeling it grate on the spine. A third quick stroke severed the head, and Nils turned and trotted for the marsh. But no orc rode out and no arrow followed him.

20.

The northmen and Finns slogged westward along the edge of the marsh until, in early afternoon, the prairie beside it ended in forest. They turned south among the trees, rested awhile and went on. When night fell, they were still walking, following game trails by instinct and moonlight. At length Nils sensed thoughts that indicated Polish conversation. Leaving his men, he approached until he could hear quiet voices and called out an Anglic. "Ahoy. We're the northmen, back from the ambush. Where is Casimir?"

A knight moved warily through the shadowed moonlight, peered closely at Nils and recognized him. "The army is scattered and Casimir is with us. I'll take you to him."

He found Casimir squatting dour and tired beside the dying embers of a fire. The king's eyes fixed him in the darkness. "Well, they're through us, and that's that. Thousands of them, about midday, riding hard. We jumped them, and it was hot and heavy for a while, but we were getting too scattered and cut up, so I had retreat blown and we fought our way back into the timber the best we could. They disengaged then and rode west down the road through the forest."

"Were they all horse barbarians, or were there orcs with them?"

The king sat silently for a few seconds as if looking at the question. "All horse barbarians. We didn't see an orc all day."

"You probably won't. I killed Kazi, and the orcs took heavy losses at the river. Without Kazi I expect they'll turn back. He was the very source of their being, and they'll be lost without him."

"Kazi dead! Then we've won after all!" Fatigue slipped from Casimir as he got to his feet. "Without him the horse barbarians will split into raiding tribes, feuding with each other, and scatter all over Europe. Given time, we can destroy them or drive them out, and rape and destruction we can recover from."

"Yes," said Nils, grinning in the moonlight. "And you can bet the western kings will get their share of fighting now."

During the next few days the allied forces regathered and recovered. Knights counted bodies while northmen and Finns scoured the countryside rounding up the horses of the dead, replenished their stock of arrows, and smoked racks of horsemeat over fires. A head count showed nineteen hundred allied cavalry able to ride but fewer than four hundred dead or badly wounded, leaving about a hundred unaccounted for. One of the dead was the gangling Jan Rezske. The bodies of nearly six hundred horse barbarians were tallied.

The northmen had lost seventy-eight and the Finns nine.

It was dusk. Zoltan Kossuth and Kuusta Suomalainen squatted on the ground with Nils, a psi tuner beside them on a fallen tree. Nils was giving Raadgiver a resume of the fighting, ending with Kazi's death and the westward movement of the horse barbarians, bypassing the allied forces. "There'll be some ugly fighting yet, and the western kings can't rely on the Slavs to do it for them any longer. You need to hold the western armies together now, especially the French."

"And what will your northmen do?"

"We're going back to northern Poland until our people have finished landing. They have only freeholders there to protect them. We'll see more fighting yet. Then we'll go to Kazi's land, or the others will. I'll follow them later, with a little luck."

Briefly Raadgiver's mind boggled. The ragtag northern tribes with only twelve hundred warriors surviving were deliberately going to Kazi's land. And without their guiding genius. So Kazi was dead; his empire still was powerful. The old psi felt a wash of dismay: they would do this in the face of sure destruction, yet seemingly with full confidence! It threatened his reality.

"My people are more able than you think," Nils responded calmly, "and you overrate my importance to them. As for myself, I know the woman I want to live with and have children by. She is one of the kinfolk. I'm going to Bavaria to find her."

Kuusta interrupted. "Are you going alone, Nils? The country'll be dangerous with horse barbarians.

I'd like to stay with my people, but if you need a companion . . ."

"I don't expect to go alone," Nils replied with a grin. "When I mention it around, some of my people will offer to go with me."

—

The next morning the northmen started west with their new horse herd.

BUT MAINLY
BY CUNNING

1.

The four neoviking warriors walked their horses easily along the dirt wagon road through the woods. Although their eyes moved alertly, they seemed neither tense nor worried.

The leaves had fallen from the beeches and rowans, but firs were master in these low Bavarian mountains, shading the road from the haze-thinned October sun of Old Wives' Summer. A shower had fallen the day before, and tracks of a single wagon showed plainly in the dirt, but around and sometimes on them were the marks of unshod hooves. It was the hoof prints that had sharpened the riders' eyes and stilled their voices. Independently they judged that nine men had followed the wagon, and none of the four felt any need to state the obvious.

Topping a rise, they saw the hoof tracks stretch out, where the riders ahead had begun to run their horses, and in a short distance the wagon tracks began to swerve, where the animal that pulled it had been whipped to a gallop. The northmen quickened their own horses' pace and, rounding a curve, saw the overturned wagon ahead.

Its driver lay beside it, blood crusted on his split skull. His horse was gone. The northmen circled without dismounting, looking down and around. Two cloaks lay beside the wagon, one large and one smaller. The tracks of the raiders' horses left the road.

The four conversed briefly in their strongly tonal language. "Less than an hour," Nils said. "Maybe as little as half an hour. With any luck they'll stop to enjoy the woman, and we'll catch them off their horses with their weapons laid aside." He rode into the woods then, eyes on the layer of fresh leaf-fall ahead, and the others followed, grinning.

The tracks led them into a deep ravine, dense with fir and hornbeam, a trickling rivulet almost lost among the stones and dead leaves in the bottom. After drinking, they slanted up the other side and followed a ridge top where pines and birch clumps formed an open stand. They continued along the crest for about five kilometers, and the tracks showed that the raiders had not stopped except, like themselves, to drink.

"Look!" Leif Trollsverd spoke quietly but clearly, without stopping his horse, pointing down the slope on the east side of the ridge. Angling toward the top was another line of tracks, of leaves scuffed and indented by hooves. The northmen quickened their mounts again until the second set of tracks joined those they'd been following. Sten Vannaren, who was in the lead now, slid from his saddle and walked back down the second set, half-bent.

"At least five," he said. "Maybe eight or nine. Hard to tell in the leaves." He came back and swung his big frame into the saddle again. "Looks as if they came along after the others had passed." He urged his horse ahead, leaning forward and looking past its neck. "And look. Here they trotted their horses as if to catch up."

He stopped and looked back. "What now, Nils?"

The blond giant stared ahead thoughtfully for a moment. "They are more of the same, and enough to let be."

Sten, somewhat the oldest of the four, nodded and swung his horse off the trail. Without further words they urged their horses at an angle, south-eastward down the ridge side.

They had ridden several kilometers through cleared farmland, the road now rutted by wagons, when they saw the village ahead, the bulk of a small castle standing a short distance past it. The huts were typical—of logs, with thatched roofs. As the road entered it, they saw that here the peasants were bolder. They didn't scurry away as had those at the smaller clusters of huts between there and the forest, although they still drew back from the road. Beside the inn the stable boy gawked at them until a brusque word jerked him to duty, and looking back over his shoulder, he led their horses into the stable.

The rim of the sun was an intense liquid bead on the forested ridge top to the west when they pushed open a door and entered the subdued light and complex smells of the small inn. The babble of conversation thinned to one beery voice, and then that face too turned toward the large barbaric-looking foreigners. The place fell still except for the slight, soft sound of their bare feet and the sounds from the kitchen. They steered toward one of the unoccupied tables, Nils's eyes scanning the room looking for the psi. He spotted him, a solitary young man sitting near the wall, the hood of his homespun brethren cloak, faded dark-green, thrown back from a lean, strong-boned face. His eyes, like everyone else's, were on them. His mind was on Nils, recognizing his psi, and suddenly started in recognition. He knew of this barbarian, had been given a mental image of him by someone with whom he shared special affinity.

"You are Ilse's next oldest brother," Nils thought.

"Yes, I am Hannes. And you're Nils, the northman who came to her hut after the Great Storm, the one she had foreseen in a premonition."

Nils's mild, calm mind validated his knowing.

"Stories have passed among the kinfolk about the things you've done since then, you and your people. Incredible stories. Is it true that you yourself killed Baalzebub?"

The innkeeper was standing beside the table. Nils ordered for himself, scarcely pausing in his silent conversation. Sten ordered for the other two, who spoke no Anglic.

"Yes, I killed Kazi, or Baalzebub, if you prefer. Now I've come to find Ilse."

"She's had your child."

The northman's mind did not react. It was a datum.

"And she's still at her hut."

"That's not good," Nils responded calmly. "There are horse barbarians in the hills."

Now that the alarming-looking strangers were sitting quietly, the peasants had returned to their conversations and beer. Suddenly Nils began to speak aloud, in Anglic, so that they could hear, while Sten interpreted in an undertone for the other two warriors. "Brother Hannes! The horse barbarians have come to the district—a strong force of them, we believe. They are scouting the country-side from the hills. What defenses are there here?"

Across the room the sun-browned psi stood up slowly, surprised by this unexpected speech. Con-versations had died abruptly as worried faces turned toward the neovikings. Hannes spoke care-fully so that the peasant with the most uncertain knowledge of Anglic could follow his words. "The baron here is Martin Gutknekt. He is a mild and honest lord, but well known for his skill at arms. He keeps a dozen knights, and since the battle on the Elbe he's kept a few dozen other armed men at the castle as well."

"And who will protect the peasants if the horse barbarians come suddenly, like rabid wolves with curved swords for teeth, to attack the villages? Maybe a hundred or more of them?" Nils's mind caught the shock of fear from the peasants.

Irritation flashed through Hannes. "Why did you say that? It was vicious," his mind accused. But as he thought it, he realized there had been no tinge of viciousness or sadism in the northman's mind. And the character pattern he read would not sup-port that interpretation. But he neither corrected himself nor apologized. Either would be redun-dant to another psi. Instead, he stood there, gazing with his mind at Nils's. "Ilse described what you are like," he said at last. "Now I see more clearly what she meant."

Nils smiled slightly, and as the innkeeper approached with roast meat and a stew of vegetables, he returned to the point. "We've seen signs of two bunches, one of nine and the other possibly as large. They behaved more like scouting parties than like vagrant bands. They didn't even stop to rape the woman they caught." His mind pictured the wagon for Hannes, with the two cloaks and the dead man, a picture more precise than any intentional memory Hannes had ever seen. It was as if the northman had complete access to his memory bank and his subconscious. His sister's mind was the finest he'd ever seen before, but it wasn't like this one.

Nils's calm thoughts continued relentlessly. "That suggests a strong force of them nearby. And they are fighters by nature. As individuals they're as good as your knights. A village is a better place to winter than in the forest, and they're reckless men. If there are as many as fifty of them, they can easily take and hold the village against the force your baron has. The knights are far too few to drive them out, and outside the castle walls the men-at-arms are no match at all for horse barbarians. Will the castle hold all the peasants?"

Hannes' mind thickened in the face of the problem. It had been generations since there had been such a need, and castles had not grown with the population.

Night had fallen and the air already felt frosty. The moon was two nights past full and would not rise for a while. In the darkness the northmen rode slowly on the short stretch of unfamiliar road between village and castle. Their horses' hooves, thudding softly on the earth, emphasized the stillness now that summer's night sounds had passed. In front of them the castle stood black against a star-strewn sky. Only a few windows in the gate tower showed lights above the wall.

Nils reached out and sensed the minds of the gate guards. As he came beneath the wall, he was near enough to see the spots on the cards through their eyes and the rough plank table. He sensed thoughts and voices in German without knowing their meaning, felt their emotions which were quiet and poorly defined. At the gate he drew his sword and hammered the hilt sharply against the timbers three times, calling in Anglic, "Open the gate."

The immediate responses were starts and flashes of irritation, followed by suspicion, probably with the realization that the hail had not been in German. Nils could not read the German thoughts, but his mind presumed them. Except for the Brethren and foreigners, who would hail in Anglic? And would one of the Brethren ever use such a pre-emptory tone? A torch was held over the battlement and a dim face looked down from an embrasure more than twenty feet above them. "Who are you and what do you want?"

"We're northmen come to see Martin Gutknekt. Let us in!"

"Come back tomorrow when the gate is open."

Nils pounded again, almost violently, bellowing, "Open! Open!"

"Peace, peace," the voice hissed from above. "If your racket disturbs the baron, you'll wish you hadn't got in. I can't let armed men in at night, unknown men, without his leave. Why can't you wait until morning?"

"Two reasons," said Nils, his voice suddenly mild.

"First, northmen don't wait unless they want to, although they'll wait forever if it suits them." With each mention of "northmen" the man's mind had reacted, Nils noted. Apparently stories of them had reached here from the war in the Ukraine and were known by more than the Brethren. He continued. "The second reason: we have information for your baron of horse barbarians near here. We will either tell him what we know right now, or we'll leave and your blood can mark your ignorance. Your scurfy district here means nothing to us that we should cool our heels."

Sten grinned at Nils, chuckling in his throat as the torch was withdrawn, and spoke softly in the northern tongue until their companions too wore wolfish grins. Then they waited silently for a span of minutes. At length Nils sensed the gateman approaching with others, one of them hard and especially self-assured. The baron, or perhaps his marshal if he had a marshal.

A narrow gate opened beside the main gate, and the gateman beckoned to them. It was almost too narrow for a horse to pass through, and low enough that the northmen dismounted to enter. The other three loosened their swords in their scabbards cautiously, but Nils, finding no treachery in the waiting minds, had taken his horse's reins and preceded them. Inside the wall the tunnel-like gateway was no wider, and where it opened into the courtyard there was another gate, a raised door of heavy bars. In the courtyard a cluster of knights waited, dimly seen. Nils's glance counted eight, and he looked at the one whom he sensed was the leader.

"Come," the man said curtly and, turning, led them, the other knights falling in behind.

The keep loomed in the darkness, perhaps twenty meters in diameter and several levels of rooms in height. Probably with a dungeon below ground level, Nils decided.

Martin Gutknekt's audience chamber was small, in keeping with his position as one of the lesser nobility. He was a freckled, small-boned man of medium height, but chunky and strong-looking. Although he met them seated, the elevation of his chair allowed him to meet Nils's eyes on the level.

"So you are northmen. The Saxons told us of your feats against the enemy far away in the east. They also told us you were going south from there into unknown lands. What are northmen doing in Bavaria?"

"I've been in Bavaria before, as a wanderer. Now we've come to find a seeress who saved my life after the Great Storm. We plan to winter in the land of the Magyars and then pass down the Donau to the sea, where our people are going."

"To the land of Baalzebub? Then it is true what we heard. You must be great fighters indeed to have defeated his army and killed him."

"No others can match our weapon skills. But there were a lot of the enemy; we won mainly by cunning. Now Baalzebub's orcs are dead or fled, and the last I saw his head, it was lying beside a Ukrainian Marsh a full meter from his neck. But his horse barbarians are still plundering, in spite of the beating you people gave them at Elbestät,

and you don't need to go farther than the hills
west of this valley to find some."

"My man told me you had news of horse barbarians near the district. Where, and how many?"

Nils described what they had seen and what
they had made of it, and the baron indicated his
acceptance of their interpretation by not disputing
it. "But they can't take the castle," he answered.
"A few score men can hold it against hundreds,
unless the hundreds have siege engines."

"They don't need the castle."

"But they can be driven out of the village."

"Not by you. There aren't enough of you."

For just an instant Gutknekt realized that the
comment should have irritated him and hadn't.
"My lord the graf can drive them out. His vassals
include three barons besides myself, plus his own
knights."

"How many men?"

The baron grew thoughtful. Five dozen knights,
perhaps, and bowmen to support them. We all
took losses at Elbestät. In fact, the old graf himself
died there, and his cousin is the graf now."

"Five dozen? Not enough," Nils said, sensing the
same thought in the baron's mind. "Not if the
horse barbarians number as many as a hundred."

"But the graf could get help from others."

"How long would it take that help to get here?"

"Two weeks, maybe less. We could easily hold
out that long."

"You could. But what about the peasants? Could
you bring them all inside the walls and shelter
and feed them? The weather can turn bad any
time now. The horse barbarians will take the
village, kill the men and take the women captive.

And if an army comes to relieve you, and it's strong enough, they may not even stay to fight. They may ride into the mountains and come back when the graf has left, or go somewhere else and take another village. That's what I'd do."

"And what do you want me to do?" The baron's voice reflected the anger of frustration that Nils read in his mind. "You say I don't have the strength to stop them, but I don't have the space to keep most of the peasants inside."

"Bring in as many as you have room for. Put sentries out with horns. Have the peasant men climb on their roofs when they hear the horns and use their bows. And give them whatever swords you can. They won't be much use to them as weapons, but they may help to stiffen their spines."

"It's against the king's law to give swords to peasants. And I can't call them men-at-arms; I already have as many as the law allows."

Nils didn't answer.

The baron sat down again, thoughtful. "Surely you don't think the peasants can hold the village." It was a statement, not a question.

"No. But there'd be fewer horse barbarians when it was over, and the peasant men, those not within the castle, will be killed anyway. It's not just a matter of this village, though. There are thousands of horse barbarians plundering through Europe, and your troubles with them won't end until they're dead or driven out. When they were in a few large armies, you marched against them, and they stood and fought and you beat them. But now that they're a lot of scattered packs, you don't know what to do about them. After Elbestät you might have kept after them and hunted them down, but you demobilized and came back to your castles to lick your wounds. Now you don't know where or when they'll strike next, or how to defend your villages. The peasants . . ."

"But would the peasants fight? They're only peasants, after all."

Nils shrugged. "Talk to the Brethren. They know the peasants better than anyone else does. There's one staying in the village now, a Brother Hannes."

Martin Gutknekt stared thoughtfully past the northmen, the discourse within his mind a slow, complex pattern of German. After a bit the brown eyes focused on Nils. "Well, Northman, I'm not used to someone else doing my thinking for me, and I'm not overly fond of it, but I thank you just the same. Will you and your friends stay here tonight? I can feed you better than they would at the inn, and the straw in the beds will be cleaner."

"Our thanks, Baron, but we'll sleep in the open. Cream draws flies. Who knows? The attack could come at sunup, and we don't want to be trapped in the inn and be butchered or in the castle and be delayed." He held out a huge hand. "We wish you luck, and the blood of your enemies."

2.

When the sun reached the meridian, the four warriors came to a crossroads. To the south they could see a larger castle in the distance. Instead of continuing in that direction, they followed the lesser road westward toward the wild forest that began with the hills. The October sun was warm, almost hot, and although they were used to wearing mail and to sweating, it felt pleasant to ride into the shade at last. At a suggestion from Leif Trollsverd they swung out of their saddles and strode along, leading their horses up the slowly climbing road, stretching their own legs, giving the animals a rest. Here the road was little more than a trail, wide enough for a wagon but humpy with stones and outcrops of bedrock.

In their own lands they were more used to going on foot or skis than on horseback, and they hiked for four hours in unbroken forest, the road curving more north than west. Soon after they'd mounted again, Nils led them off the road at a blazed tree and along a little path that led to a cabin. He held up a hand and stopped them as soon as he could see the cabin through the trees. His careful eyes saw nothing wrong. His subconscious, remembering perfectly, comparing in detail, saw nothing different that could not be accounted for by the passage of time, by the change of seasons from one winter to the following autumn. But he knew unquestionably that something was seriously the matter.

They sat without moving, all but Nils aware of the occasional movements of their horses, their eyes carefully examining the cabin and the woods around it. Their ears were alert for meaningful sound.

Nils's questing awareness assured him that no one was there now, and that it was safe. When he led them forward again, it was still with a sense of something wrong. The shutters were open, and the interior was lit by autumn sunshine filtered through thin-scraped deer hides stretched over the windows. The place had been used by horse barbarians, apparently in a rain, for one had voided in a corner. Blood had dried on the split logs of the floor. The expressions of the three mirrored their separate characters as they looked from the blood to Nils.

The blond Jöt, Erik Bärsärken, showed covert pleasure, his eyes gleaming in anticipation of vendetta. In Leif Trollsverd's darker face the jaw muscles were knotted; there was a blood debt here. Sten Vannaren, keen-minded and long on experience, merely watched his big young friend to see what his reaction might be; he had decided some time before that Nils Järnhann was a new kind of man, whose acts he could not yet predict but would in time.

Nils walked slowly through the cabin's two rooms, his eyes missing nothing. Then all four went outside and examined the ground.

"They were here yesterday, and once a few days earlier," he said at last. "Maybe some will come tonight. We'll bed within hearing, in a thicket."

As they led their horses downwind of the cabin, they smelled rotting flesh. By a clump of hazel they found the body of a baby, skull smashed, its flesh gnawed by polecats. In a draw behind the cabin they found Ilse's spring, and the tracks where horse barbarians had ridden up the brook. They staked their horses some distance away and returned, holing up in a grove of old firs ringed with sapling growth that screened them from the nearby cabin. From their saddle bags they took dried meat, cheese and hard bread, and ate without talking. When they were done, they stretched out on top of their sleeping robes and relaxed like wild animals.

Soon the sun had dropped behind the crest of the ridge in back of them. All heard the voices at the same time, loud and in a language that was not German. They lay quietly, listening to the careless sounds. This time the horse barbarians came down the draw above the spring. Soon the voices were lost within the cabin's walls.

Nils spoke for a moment in an undertone, answered by nods and narrow-eyed grins. They buckled on their harnesses, took swords, shields and bows, and slipped through the trees to where they could see the cabin clearly. It still was full daylight, even in the shadow of the ridge. The horse barbarians had tethered their horses on leather ropes, to browse the twig ends of the brush, and after a

brief intent examination of the surroundings the
northmen decided that all were inside. The smoke
of a young fire was starting from the chimney.

Each side of the cabin had openings. There
was a door in front and one in back, and each
side wall had two windows, one into each room.
Leif Trollsverd, an arrow nocked, took a position
from which he could cover the back door and the
windows in one of the side walls. Sten knelt behind a tree diagonally opposite, covering the front
and the other side. Erik slipped smoothly across
the narrow strip of open ground to the side of the
house and around the corner, stationing himself
beside the back door, his teeth exposed in an ugly
grin.

A moment later Nils appeared from the other
side. He had a dry fir branch in his right hand, one
end wrapped with blazing birch bark. As he ran
up to the wall, he threw the branch onto the shake
roof, then darted around the corner, shifting his
sword from his left hand to his right. He could
sense the sudden intentness inside; they had heard
the thump of the torch.

Just as Nils reached the side of the door, a
swarthy youth stepped out, started, jumped back,
but the sword stroke caught him as he moved and
he fell backward into the cabin with his rib cage
cloven. The short shouts from inside meant nothing to Nils, but the thoughts that reached him
were of anger and alarm. He stood shoulder to the
wall, waiting for another, but none came. There
were sounds of men scrambling, of swords being
drawn from scabbards, and Nils sensed one of
them standing by the wall, just inside the door,
waiting for someone to try an entrance.

"That's one!" Nils shouted.

They were talking inside now, urgently and with undertones of fear. Through Sten's eyes, Nils saw flames begin to blaze up around the torch, but those inside were not aware of it yet because of the loft that separated them from the roof. From the rear of the cabin a brief clashing of steel sounded.

"Make that two!" came Erik's cheerful bellow.

Through the eyes of the man inside the door, Nils watched a lean youth draw a knife, slash the sides and top of one of the window coverings, and thrust his head and shoulders through. Uttering a bleating cry he fell backwards, and with a convulsive jerk pulled an arrow from the muscles of his neck. He rolled over onto hands and knees, retching, blood gushing from the wound and from his open mouth, then collapsed forward on his face. With an abrupt roar, another man ran and hurled himself headlong through the open window. Rounding the corner he ran at Nils, drawing his sword, fell forward to his knees, rose slowly, and fell again as a second arrow drove through his mail shirt.

Nils's mind counted the consciousnesses inside. "That's four," he shouted. "Two for Sten. There are six left." A victorious whoop came from Sten's position among the trees.

Inside, too, there was talk, and one horse barbarian stationed himself by each window and door. Their tough minds broadcast uncertainty, with various mixtures of anger and fear. They had no clear idea of what they were up against and no concerted idea of what to do beyond defending themselves. Again through Sten's eyes, Nils watched the flames on the roof, burning higher now and starting to spread.

Suddenly there was a mental shock of alarm from inside, then quick words of instruction. One of the window guards left his post, and Nils's mind went with him up the ladder, raising the trapdoor and gazing into the dark loft. Above he saw the bright flames burning through the roof. At that moment some burning material fell near him and the man dropped from the ladder to the floor below, yelling.

A few hoarse words drew them all into the front room; Nils in turn shouted to Erik. All six rushed for the open door. Nils's stroke caught the first as he emerged, sweeping below the shield and cutting his legs from under him. The second hurdled him before Nils could strike again, and attacked with berserk rage while a third ran out behind him. From inside came oaths and grunts as Erik fell on them from behind. Sten put an arrow through the third man out while Nils killed his furious assailant and went crouched through the door to help Erik.

Erik needed no help. One lay struck dead from behind and a second was down, bleeding and helpless, cursing. The blond Jöt stood watching through the open window; the last of the enemy patrol had jumped through it and was running into the woods, holding his right shoulder where an arrow was embedded. A grinning, red-haired figure pursued him out of sight among the trees. In a minute Sten reappeared, waving his bloody sword, and they left the burning cabin.

When Nils's eyes opened, they focused first on the skeletal crown of a naked beech, its major limbs dimly resolved against the night sky. A few stars of larger magnitude were visible between the black masses of fir tops, and moving his head, he could see the lopsided moon past the meridian, telling him that dawn wasn't far off. Its pale light washed patches of ground and filled others with dense black shadow. Forty meters away, between the stems of trees and brush, he could see dull red where the collapsed heap of the cabin still smoldered. Its smell was strong but not unpleasant. Frost from his breath coated the fur at the upper edge of his sleeping robe.

He had wakened wide, not from the cold or the moonlight but from something that lay calm and watchful in his mind. Without ever having experienced it before, he knew it was the consciousness of a he-wolf, probably one of Ilse's familiars, but he didn't know how to communicate with it.

The wolf had sensed his waking telepathically and had waited until Nils was aware of him. As if it had sensed Nils's psi power even when the northman was still asleep—as if it had recognized what being was there. And then it held a picture of Ilse in its mind for Nils to see. The picture zoomed in on Ilse's face and seemed to go right into her mind where there was a physical and mental image of Nils. And with that as an almost instantaneous background, the picture was again of Ilse, hands tied, being taken away by a patrol of horse barbarians. As Nils sat up in his sleeping furs, the picture became one of a large man, Nils, on horseback, with undefined representations of companions, following a large wolf through the forest.

The picture faded and the emission of the wolf's

mind changed to a quiet formlessness, as Ilse said his own did. Nils acknowledged, then lay back down and went to sleep almost at once, not to awake again until the gray wash of dawn.

He wakened his companions and the four warriors squatted hunched beneath their robes, silently gnawing cheese and dry bread, bodies stiff with cold and sleep. The only speech was Nils's quiet voice. They were glad to lead their horses up the dim slope to the ridge crest; the exertion warmed them before they mounted and rode away.

When the sun was two hours high, they lay beneath the low branches of a thicket of sapling firs. Farther downslope a fire had consumed the undergrowth two or three years earlier, leaving an open clumpy stand of older trees. A good campsite. Forty-two teepeelike tents stood on the gentle toe-slope—more than one hundred men and perhaps close to two hundred. Secure in their strength and hidden site, the horse barbarians had become careless again about sentries.

"Leif, run down there and bloody your sword," Erik breathed with a grin. "We did all the work yesterday."

Trollsverd grunted an obscenity.

Sten chuckled. "That's the price of a big reputation; they kept away from him. And when did fighting start to be work?"

Nils ignored their whispered chaffing. They were within the range of normal telepathic pickup from the camp—close enough that loud voices could be heard. He had intended to reach Ilse with his mind, but now he did not dare a forceful telepathic call to get her attention. For there were two psi minds in the camp—hers and one that belonged to a horse barbarian.

"This place is dangerous," he whispered. "There's a psi down there." With that they wriggled back out of the thicket and slipped away.

3.

The castle was much larger than that of Martin Gutknekt and had a moat with brown billows of dead algae. The gate stood open in the sunlit morning as the neovikings walked their horses across the drawbridge. The gate guards scowled at the strangely garbed and equipped riders but did not move to stop them. As the warriors approached the great squat keep, the two guards at its entrance lowered their pikes, and one called down to halt. "Who are you, and what do you want?"

Nils stared up the stone steps at them, one enormous hand spread on a thick thigh, making the most of his size and imposing physique as they stared back at him. "Who is your master?" he responded.

This question for a question stopped the slow-witted guard. After a moment he answered, "The graf, Karl Haupmann."

"Tell him four northmen are here to see him, with information about a strong force of horse barbarians in the country."

The sun-browned face stared suspiciously at

the big northman, jaws working with indecision.
These strangers obviously were not nobles, or even
knights. Nils helped him. "Or would you rather be
staked out in the sun and flayed?"

The guard stepped back, then turned reluctantly
through the open door. His partner's mind squirmed
with discomfort at being left alone to face the four
big warriors, a discomfort that the three could
read in his face as certainly as Nils read it in his
mind.

"At home men like that would be thralls," Leif
Trollsverd said.

"That's about what they are here," Sten answered.

The remaining guard stared at them, perplexed
by the unfamiliar tonal syllables. He knew German and Anglic, but had never heard any other
language and was uncertain whether this was truly
speech or not. After several minutes a burly knight
came out of the interior and squinted down at
them in the bright sunshine. He snapped fast words
in German, and they sat looking impassively up at
him until he repeated in Anglic. "Who are you,
and what do you want?"

"We are northmen and want to see the graf,"
Nils said dryly. "We've seen a large force of horse
barbarians near the district of Martin Gutknekt."

The knight sneered. "Show a skin-clad savage a
peasant riding on an ox and there's no telling
what he'll think he saw."

The usually imperturbable Sten rose in his stirrups and had his sword half out before Nils put a
hand on his wrist and spoke softly in Swedish.
Turning back to the knight, Nils said with mild

calm, "Then let us tell him what we think we saw."

Without saying anything more, the man led them inside and to a throne room some fifteen meters long. Entering, they passed two guards with pikes and swords who stood by the open door. Five mail-clad knights stood on the dais near the throne; three were breathing deeply as if they had hurried to be there. Karl Haupmann sat upright and hard-faced, as his marshal, followed by the barbaric-looking warriors, strode to the foot of the dais and stated the particulars in German.

Nils recognized an unforeseen problem here. The graf was a cruel and ruthless man with a pathological suspicion of foreigners.

He looked at them. "Northmen, eh? What is this about horse barbarians?"

"There's a large force of them, between one and two hundred, camped in the mountains near the district of Martin Gutknekt. We think they plan to take his principal village."

The graf's emotional pattern was ugly, but his speech, if curt, was civil. "Why do you think they'll try to take Doppeltanne?"

Nils sensed here a xenophobe who might have them attacked on the spot if he thought it safe. And lacking any tactical advantage, the odds of nine to four did not appeal to Nils, especially with the two door guards behind them. He stated his answer matter-of-factly, in a voice of utter assurance. "First, I didn't say 'try.' There is no question of their ability. Second, they'll need food and shelter for the winter, and the village has both. Third, they're camped near Gutknekt's district. And forth, they're in tents, making no effort to build huts against the winter."

"And why should I listen to you?" The graf's control cracked for a moment. "You are foreign barbarians yourselves. What are northmen doing in Bavaria, unless . . .?"

"We're going to Baalzebub's land. Our army beat his and killed Baalzebub himself. Now we will take his country."

"But we'd heard you were passing far to the east, far east of the Czechlands." The graf stared intently at Nils through narrowed eyes.

"The rest of our people are. The four of us have come this way to see to some business."

"What business?"

To say "a woman" might amuse and relax the graf, but it might also make them seem ludicrous and weak. On the other hand, while to say "our own business" might offend him dangerously, it might also impress him with their fearlessness and make him cautious.

"Our own business."

The graf darkened and, turning, spoke to his marshal in German for a full minute. The marshal nodded curtly and left. The other knights tightened.

"Then why do you come to tell me about horse barbarians? They're no business of yours, are they?" There was a note of triumph in the graf's voice.

"Maybe they shouldn't be. Not here at any rate." Nils looked at the others. "Let's go," he said in Swedish, "but be ready to fight." They turned to leave.

"Wait!" The graf stood up. "You saw their camp. How can we find it?"

They stopped. "It is in the mountains west of

Doppeltanne," Nils answered. There are three main ridges between the valley and their camp, or maybe four. They are camped along the east foot of the next ridge west. Or they were. They may be in Doppeltanne by now."

The man was stalling for time, Nils realized.

Sitting back down, the graf asked more questions about the condition of the enemy and their horses and what Nils thought their tactics might be. After several minutes he arose abruptly. "I am keeping you from your journey," he said. "Thank you, Northmen, for your information." His eyes were like chips of flint, and a smile played at one corner of his mouth. "And travel in peace."

Nils nodded, and the four warriors started toward the tall broad door of the chamber. Halfway there Nils sensed that the knights were moving; glancing back, he saw them sauntering from the dais. Though seemingly casual, they were taut inside, and nervous. Nils paused briefly in the doorway, then started down the wide corridor.

"When he sent his marshal out," he said rapidly, "it was to set a trap. After that he was stalling for time. The ones behind us are the smaller jaw."

The short flight of stairs leading down to the entrance of the keep was only half as wide as the corridor. They would be bunched there, with no room to maneuver. Just short of the stairs, Nils quietly said "Stop," steppped to a window and leaned out on his stomach through the thick-walled opening to scan the courtyard. Outside stood a phalanx of bowmen and a group of mounted knights, facing the door.

The knights following the northmen had continued a few paces and stopped uncertainly. "Take them," Nils said, and they fell upon them.

At the sounds of fighting and the shouts of the knights, the entrance guards below began to shout. The unexpectedness and ferocity of the northmen's attack overran the knights, three of whom fell while the others gave way and let them pass. One of the guards at the throne room door dropped his pike and ran into a side corridor while the other, cursing, stepped quickly through the door and tried to close it. It burst open in his face, throwing him to the floor as the four warriors rushed in.

The graf stood in front of his throne, drawing a short sword, but Nils met him at the foot of the dais and bisected him casually in passing, then led them through a curtained doorway behind the throne and up a flight of stairs. This took them to a suite of rooms above, where they found a woman, obviously the grafin, and a boy in his early teens. Startled, the boy drew a knife, but Leif grabbed his wrist and the knife clattered on the flags as the boy yelled with pain.

Erik covered the stairwell then, and Leif and Sten held their two prisoners while Nils gagged them. They could hear someone shouting in the throne room, and while Nils snatched a bow and quiver of arrows from the wall, angry voices and shod feet sounded from below. Strong-arming their prisoners, they hurried out of the apartment into another corridor and from it into a climbing stairwell that wound within the outer wall.

Voices surged into the corridor they had just left, and Nils shouted down in Anglic to stop, that they had the grafin and the boy. Pursuit stopped, although the voices only paused, and the north-

men went on up the stairs until they emerged onto
the top of the keep. Erik and Sten strayed by the
trapdoor, tying the woman with strips of her
petticoat. Leif pushed the boy ahead of him to the
parapet and lifted him bodily into an embrasure
where he could be clearly seen, powerful fists holding him firmly by belt and jerkin. Nils laid the
bow and quiver against the parapet and leaned
through an embrasure next to the one the boy was
in.

A growing crowd stood below in the courtyard,
including some of the archers and a knight, but
their attention was on the entrance, and they had
not yet seen the figures in the embrasures above.
For a long minute things hung like that, as if the
world had slowed down, until a knight jogged shouting out of the entrance of the keep, followed by
others, and all eyes turned to the top. Briefly there
were angry shouts from the courtyard, but Nils
kept still, monitoring emotions, until a waiting
near-silence had settled. Then he spoke, loudly, so
that he was clearly heard twenty meters below.

"We came in peace to warn the graf of an army
of horse barbarians camped within the country." A
babble of voices rose that Nils waited out. "As our
reward he tried to have us murdered." He paused.
"Now he is dead, and we have his wife and boy
hostage."

Although the crowd remained quiet, Nils stopped
until he could sense unease below, and the beginning of impatience, then called down again. "Who
was the marshal of the old graf? The graf killed at
Elbestät? Step forward if you're here."

The faces below turned to a tall, square-shouldered knight who stood looking grimly upward before striding out in front of the archers.

"And the man who is marshal now. Let him step forward."

The burly, sneering knight came into the open beside the other.

Without speaking, Nils stepped back from the embrasure out of sight, nocked an arrow and bent the bow. Then, stepping to the embrasure again, he let the bowstring go and the new marshal fell with an arrow in his chest.

The crowd made a sound like a many-voiced sigh, but no one else moved. In that instant of shock Nils shouted down, "The marshal from before is now the ruler of this castle until the king names a new graf. Come up and parley with us, and then we'll leave."

4.

The northmen spent the night at the forest's edge on the eastern side of the valley, partway to Doppeltanne. At dawn they rode on, gnawing cheese and hard bread as they rode through frost-rimed grass. The timber's edge was grazed and open, alternating between heavy-limbed oaks and groves of gray beeches as hollow as chimneys, their fire-scarred bases doors to squirrels and polecats. After some hours they could see the castle of Martin Gutknekt, and then Doppeltanne. Cattle foraged in the stubble fields tended by boys with long sticks, so the neovikings rode out openly and came to the castle before noon.

The sun was warm now, and outside the walls sweating peasant youths swung swords in a clumsy parody of drill, rasped by the cutting tongue of a knight. Rapt children and glum old men stood watching. In the courtyard were dozens of peasant women squatting around small fires, preparing the noon meal. Shelters of poles, hides and woven mats were being built.

The northmen found the baron in the armory,

sparring with his marshal with shields and blunt swords. He stepped back and turned a sweating face to them. "Too damned crowded to practice in the courtyard." He wiped his face with a rag. "I thought you'd be far gone by now. Do you have any news? I sent men out yesterday, good hunters, and they found tracks."

"If they'd been with us, they'd have seen more than tracks," Nils answered. "We found their camp a few hours west of here. There are more than a hundred of them, judging by their tents. Probably closer to two hundred. We took the news to the graf, and frankly we thought we might find the village taken by now. Do you know where we might find Brother Hannes?"

"He may be in the village. We talked two days ago, and then we both talked to the peasants. Since then he's been riding around the district encouraging them, and he chose the men we issued swords to. He says they're the likeliest to fight."

"The Brethren know the people's minds as if they could see into them," Nils commented. "I'll go look for him. With your leave I'd like to talk to both of you together."

As soon as Nils rode out the gate, he sensed Hannes; he had come to watch the peasants drill. Hannes was clearly depressed; he knew that soon many of these people would die. Turning at the approach of the warriors, he sensed at once that Nils brought bad news, and guessed.

"She's dead?"

"No. Prisoner."

"Gentle Father Jakob."

After seven centuries the memory of Jakob Tashi Norbu, the Tibetan-Swiss psionicist, still was revered by the kinfolk. The lean telepath breathed his name now partly in gratitude, partly in pain.

"But I intend to get her back," Nils said. "Now let's go talk to the baron. We have plans to make."

Hannes looked at him with sudden appreciation. There seemed no emotional content to anything he had heard Nils say or think—his emotions had to be a lot different than other people's, just as his mind was. But he knew that if it wasn't for Ilse, Nils would have left his warning and been two days gone from the district by now. Hannes held up his hand to Nils and, half-jumping, half-hoisted, mounted behind the warrior.

Nils stepped back from the rough map he had drawn. "And that's where their camp is from here, as best I can show you. But they won't stay there much longer. I've never seen or heard of horse barbarians starting anything at night, although that doesn't mean they won't. There are different tribes with different tongues, and this bunch may be different from those we've had experience with. Or they may have changed their tactics since last summer. But it's my guess they'll attack by daylight. And after they take the village they'll probably get drunk. If Hannes and Sten took your armed peasants into the forest east of the valley after dark tonight and camped there . . ."

Nils, Leif and Erik ate and replenished their saddlebags, saluted Sten in casual farewell, and left. They rode several kilometers south down the road to where a finger of forest approached it on a low spur ridge from the west. Beyond it they angled southwesterly and entered the forest. This route, they hoped, would bypass possible enemy scouts. Gradually their course curved until, near sundown, they were following the upper west slope of the fourth major ridge and heading north.

The horse barbarians were raiders from the deserts, steppes and arid mountains of the Middle East, whose tradition was open-mounted attack or simple ambush. The neovikings, on the other hand, were raiders of the Scandinavian forests, whose style was cunning and stealth. And at home they'd made an important part of their living hunting on foot with bows. Thus their sensors missed little and their minds remembered and correlated what they saw and heard and smelled, like the Iroquois of twelve hundred years earlier. So this stretch of ridge was familiar to them, though they'd seen it only once before and from a different approach. After a bit they rode into the bottom of the heavily wooded valley west of the ridge and tied their horses in a stand of young fir that was littered and almost fenced by the blown-down bones of ancestors. It was not the kind of place a rider was likely to wander into.

Then, on foot and with their sleeping robes in bundles on their backs, they climbed back up the long slope as dusk began to settle, and slipped toward the enemy camp. Nils sensed no sentry. When he decided they were approaching the range of normal telepathy, he left Leif and Erik in a tangle of blowdown and moved quietly on until he was receiving the casual, though to him unintelligible, thoughts of the Turkic tribesmen nearby. After determining his line of withdrawal, he lay beside the slightly raised disk of roots and soil of a pole-sized fir that had partly uprooted and lodged

in the top of a beech. Come morning, the gap
beneath the roots would give nearly perfect concealment if needed.

His mind stilled as no other human mind could,
as indiscernible to a watchful psi as possible. Soon
it was dark, and yellow campfires danced nearby.
His body relaxed within his robe as his mind
received, correlated and stored.

After a time he permitted himself to sleep. A
unit of awareness monitored the environment to
awaken him if necessary.

At dawn he awoke without moving and let his
eyes sweep the gray-lit woods within their range,
his ears and psi sense alert, his subconscious carefully sorting sensations. He was aware that the
two psi minds in the camp were awake too, along
with many others. Ilse and the other psi were
together, but far enough from Nils that he couldn't
receive passive optical impressions from either of
them. From the male, Nils recognized the patterns
of a strong but undisciplined mind.

She was speaking Anglic to him.

The light was growing stronger. Slowly Nils slid
into the dark opening under the tipped-up roots.
Breakfast fires were being lit. Soon early-morning
taciturnity disappeared among the enemy tribesmen
as fires and movement warmed them. Their eating
took some time, and Nils could hear them talking
and laughing, the sounds mixed with the patterns
of telepathic emissions that were their natural
accompaniment.

He continued to lie there, his mind focused on
the two psis, other minds relegated to background.
He knew which tent was theirs. Then a man came
from it and the bearings of the two minds sepa-

rated as he walked through the camp. Soon men and captive women began to strike tents, rolling them into bundles. Others trailed down the gentle toe slope toward a long meadow that bordered the creek in the valley bottom and returned leading strings of horses.

Nils saw Ilse then, pulling down the tent, folding and rolling it. The man returned when she was done and helped load it on a horse. Within an hour all gear had been loaded. The horse barbarians mounted, their voices lively and boisterous at the prospect of action. The psi led them in a loose column through the trees, eastward toward Doppeltanne. Pack animals, spare mounts and colts followed. A score of women sat the nags of the string bareback, waiting while the pack train moved out. Behind them were mounted guards.

By the time the women started moving, the chief of the band was perhaps a kilometer ahead. Nils called to Ilse telepathically. She did not turn; only her mind responded.

"Nils!"

"Are they going to attack Doppeltanne?"

She wrenched her mind to the question. "Yes. And be careful. He's a psi you know, and he understands a fair amount of Anglic; he's been learning it since Poland." She began to ride more slowly, letting most of the women pass, until one of the rearguard shouted at her and gestured with his lance.

"I'll try to get you free tonight," Nils thought after her.

"Don't take chances. Perhaps I know how to kill him."

"Tonight," his thought followed her. "We'll make

our move tonight." He watched her out of sight.
The information should be safe with her, if she'd
been able to submerge and screen well enough to
work out a murder scheme without her captor
reading it. One of Kazi's psi officers must have
discovered the man's potential and had him trained,
as Raadgiver had done with him. Operational
telepaths very rarely just happened.

Several tents remained. Two women worked
around them, and two guards sat beside a fire,
talking and laughing. A man came from one of the
tents, helping himself with a crutch. Very carefully Nils moved from his post toward the hiding
place of his companions. Softly though he moved,
his approach awakened Erik, whose hand moved
quickly to his sword as he sat up. Leif grinned. "I
let the growing boy sleep late," he said softly in
his lilting Norwegian.

"They've broken camp," Nils said, "and they're
riding toward Doppeltanne. They left some wounded
behind, with a pair of women to look after them,
and a couple of guards. We'll get our horses and
then ride in and take them."

The northmen hiked over the ridge top and down
to their horses, saddled them and fastened the bits
in their mouths, all without hurry. Then they rode
back and walked their horses toward the camp.

When one of the guards heard their approach
and looked their way, they kicked their mounts
into a gallop and cut the men down while they
scrambled for their bows. One of the women half-
choked a scream and then both stood by, frightened.
These savage foreigners in deerskin breeches and
black mail, with bare-fanged totems on their

helmets, seemed just a different variety of horse barbarian. While Erik sat with arrow on bowstring, covering, Nils and Leif rode around cutting the lodgepoles with their heavy swords and knocking down tents. As the occupants ducked or crawled out or lay humped beneath the hides, they were killed.

One stared as Nils charged at him, a shock of recognition on his dark, scarred face, and Nils reined hard left to avoid trampling the man. A picture had flashed through the horse barbarian's mind, of this same giant warrior with straw-colored braids standing naked and weaponless in an arena, stalked by a grinning orc officer with sword in hand. It was this man, Nils realized, who had thrown his own curved sword down onto the sand.

"Let that one be!" Nils shouted, and left the man on hands and knees beside his crutch while they finished their killing.

The women stared in shock and fear as Nils turned his horse and looked at them. "Can you ride?" he asked in Anglic.

They nodded dumbly.

"Then get on those horses. Ride to the top of that ridge and go in that direction." He pointed. "Do you understand?" They nodded again. "Stay on top of the ridge until you come to a road. It will take two or three hours or maybe more. When you come to the road, ride down the road with the sun on your right shoulder. Your *right* shoulder. When you come out of the forest, you'll soon arrive at a crossroads. From there you can see a castle. Go to the castle. Tell them that the enemy is in

Doppeltanne. Doppeltanne! Now tell me what I said."

Hesitantly and with help they repeated his instructions, then walked to the horses and rode away, glancing back repeatedly until they were out of sight.

"Think they'll get lost?" Leif asked.

"I don't think so," Nils answered. "They had the directions well enough." Then he turned and looked at the man he'd spared.

The stocky barbarian stood now, staring at them, not knowing what to expect. He didn't imagine that Nils knew who he was. He'd been one among tens of thousands shouting in the stands, and when he'd thrown the sword, the giant had been looking the other way.

Nils dismounted and walked over to him. "You gave me a chance to live," he said. "Now we are even." The Swedish words meant nothing to the man, but the tone was not threatening. The other northmen looked at each other. Nils jabbed the man lightly on the shoulder with a thick, sword-callused forefinger, then pointed to the man's side where his sword would have hung. Next he moved as if drawing a sword and made a throwing movement. Pointing to himself, he bent as if to take something from the ground, then held out his hand as if armed. The man stared with awed understanding.

Nils remounted then and they rode leisurely to the meadow where the horse barbarians had kept their horse herd. There the northmen hobbled their mounts and let them graze until after noon, while they napped in the autumn sun.

5.

It was night. The horse barbarians had loosed their horses in a field fenced on three sides with rails and on the fourth with a tight hedge. The fence wasn't high enough to hold horses like theirs, so they had hobbled them.

Their chief had posted four guards on horseback to patrol outside the paddock, and they were disgusted to be pulling guard duty while they could hear the drunken shouts from the village. So when buddies sneaked out to them with two jugs of schnapps, they didn't hesitate. It wasn't as if vigilance was needful. The fighting men in this land had all the stealth of a cattle herd.

Dismounting, they tethered their mounts to the fence and squatted down together with their backs against it to test the schnapps. The chief, they agreed, would be too busy enjoying himself to check on them. Or if he did, it was very dark and the moon wouldn't rise until after midnight. They'd be able to hear him before he found them.

The three northmen lay in the tall grass at the

edge of a ditch, listening to their murmuring and quiet laughter.

He had read his peasants well, Hannes realized. The thirty he'd chosen, most of them youths, had more violence simmering in them than he'd realized they could generate, partly a result of being armed. To strenghen their anger, he had purposely moved them close enough, shortly after the village had been taken, to hear the shouts and occasional screams. Then he'd pulled them back, for Nils had warned him that one of the horse barbarians was a psi. Probably their chief, Hannes decided. Now he listened to the thoughts and emotions of his men. Some were angry enough that they were not even nervous, only impatient. A few were managing to doze, but the night was too cold here behind the hedge to sleep soundly, and their homespun blankets were not for out-of-doors.

He looked at the big northman beside him. Sten. The face was turned eastward. Occasional patterns in unintelligible Swedish drifted through the man's mind, with fragmentary and partially visualized scenes, but mostly the neoviking's mind was nearly motionless, though awake and quietly serene. To a degree it reminded Hannes of a cat they'd had at home when he was a boy. Or of Nils.

At the thought of Nils he turned and looked westward past the village toward the low black mass of mountains defined against gleaming stars. Had the three northmen survived their scouting expedition? Had they found the paddock? If they hadn't . . . Shivering partly with cold, he tried to shake off the line of thinking, but thoughts of death

came back to him. If they had died or otherwise
failed their mission, the rest of them would be
dead by morning. Except perhaps Sten; Sten might
escape.

Would Sten feel grief if his three friends were
killed? There was clearly strong affinity between
them. Yet somehow Hannes didn't think Sten
would. It would be like his cat, when he'd been a
boy. She'd loved her kittens, in her way, and de-
fended them, but when one was killed, she'd sniffed
it and then walked casually away without sorrow.
That was how it would be with Sten; Sten was
somewhat like Nils.

Nils. Someday the big psi-warrior would die,
probably violently, but somehow he didn't believe he
was dead yet.

Zühtü Hakki lay on his side on the straw-filled
tick, staring through the darkness at the dim form
of the woman on the heap of hay across the room.
She lay still, but her mind was awake, her thoughts
an unintelligible mental murmuring in German.
From somewhere outside he heard coarse laughter.
Drunk, every mother's son of them probably. Probably even the paddock guards. All but Mustafa and
his detail. It's a good thing the enemy are all
bottled up inside the castle, he thought. Old Mustafa
will keep his boys sober and in the saddle, and the
dogs in the castle won't try to sally out past that
pack of wolves. Mustafa never drinks. The older
men say he never did. Wonder why? Almost un-
heard of, a man who doesn't drink. Besides Mustafa
I'm probably the only man here who's voluntarily
sober, and I've had a pull or two. Funny that since

my psi was trained, I've had no desire to get drunk.
Other desires, but not to get drunk. He opened his
eyes again and looked toward the woman. There
were prettier women; plump ones. But I'll stick
with this one. You can get tired of a pretty woman,
but this one has a mind. Funny. Until my psi was
trained, I never cared if a woman had a mind. And
tonight she'd been different. No wonder I'm tired.
*Very tired. Loose and relaxed and very, very tired.
And safe here. Very safe here. Very safe and very
secure. My eyes are heavy. Very, very heavy. They
keep wanting to close. Can't keep them open any
more. No need to. Now they're closed. And I can't
open them. Couldn't open them if I tried. Don't want
to try. Sleepy. Very sleepy. Very, very sleepy. I'm falling asleep. Falling deeply asleep. Deeply asleep. It
feels so good to fall deeply, deeply asleep.*

Ilse kept the thoughts running through her/his
mind, surrounding them with full, soft inner feelings and pictures of sinking through clouds. She
took him deeper and deeper. *And now I can't move,*
her mind murmured. *Don't want to move. Can't
move. Very peaceful here, and I refuse to move, or
see, or hear, or feel.*

She continued this briefly. Then she rose quietly,
rolled the comatose chieftain off the straw tick
and pulled his war harness from under it. And
usually, she thought, he sleeps as lightly as a cat.
The curved sword was not heavy and her arms
were strong. There was light enough from the dying
fire. She kept her eyes on the neck and swung
hard, then, with a shudder, threw the blade on the
tick and wiped her hands on her greasy homespun
skirt, although there was no blood on them. Her

mind shifted outside where it found a drunken guard sleeping on the cold doorstone. Fumbling in the gloom, she got the knife sheath off the harness and fastened it to the strip of homespun that served her as a belt.

Then she opened the shutters on a side window and climbed out. A peasant body lay beneath it, where it had fallen from the roof during the brief afternoon battle, and she stumbled on it. A ladder still leaned against the thatched eaves. She climbed it and huddled grimly against the stone chimney.

A few men could be heard, or sensed, still wandering or staggering between the huts or down the village street. She heard the sound of violent vomiting, followed by roars of laughter. But most of them were inside now, out of the cold, sleeping. She could barely sense their sleeping minds through the log walls.

It wouldn't do to be here when the sun rises, she thought. If nothing happens by the time the moon is halfway to the meridian, I'll have to try to get away by myself.

Two of the horse guards had fallen asleep and the other two squatted murmuring and laughing. They were too dulled to hear the bowstrings. One slumped to his side. The other rose unsteadily to his knees, looking stupidly at the arrow in his belly, then fell forward.

When they had finished with them, the northmen pulled down the top rails from a section of fence, throwing them out of the way. Then they mounted three of the guards' horses and rode them into the paddock. The animals there were conditioned to the smell of blood and sounds of death, and for a while they didn't take alarm as the warriors quietly walked their mounts around, casually killing horses with their swords. After a little they spooked, however, milling in the darkness, and the northmen worked faster. Some found the place where the fence had been lowered, and Erik stationed himself there as guard and executioner. It didn't take them long to panic then, hopping clumsily in their hobbles and whinnying in the light of the half-risen moon.

The reddish moon, shaved to slightly less than half a disk, had risen almost entirely above the hills, throwing a pale light over the valley. The sentry atop the gate tower strained his eyes northward. Something was going on over there with the enemy's horses, but it was much too far to see by moonlight. The swine outside heard it, too, he thought. One of them was shouting orders, and three trotted their horses down the road in that direction.

When the first limb of the moon had shown, he had hissed the news down to the courtyard, and the knights had mounted their horses. The sounds of their low voices had stopped, and they sat in hard and silent readiness. All he could hear now was the occasional impatient sound of a hoof stamping on the packed ground or a creak of leather.

Suddenly there was another sound, startling him, distant shouts and whoops, as of horsemen riding into the village from the east. The enemy outside turned, staring in that direction but unable to see a thing except the buildings standing dimly in the moonlight across the fields. Their captain trotted his horse a few tentative steps in that direction, stopped for a brief moment, then spoke a command. The whole body of them broke into a gallop toward the village.

The sentry called down quietly and heard the dull sound of well-greased chains as the portcullis was raised. The gates opened and the knights trotted out, then spurred their horses forward.

Sten led the peasant charge, and just outside the village his whoop signalled theirs to begin. Briefly they stormed through the village, chopping at the occasional enemy caught outside, before those inside roused and began to stumble o' t of doorways. Sten knew there was nothing like danger to clear the fumes from a drunken brain, but still, the enemy was afoot, confused, and slow of reflexes, and the clumsy hate-filled peasants rode hewing among the huts.

Then, more quickly than he'd expected, the angry, sober troop that had stood watch outside the castle were on them, and he shouted and heard Hannes shout to ride, ride for the forest. Peasant bloodlust turned to panic before the onslaught, and they fled, or tried to, streaming out into the field with clots of horse barbarians cutting them out of their saddles. Wishing he were the horseman the enemy were, Sten drew alongside Hannes, guarding him because the man was something to Nils.

The knights had bypassed the village to the east. There were only twelve of them, but they were strong and battle-hardened and they hit as a solid wave, unexpectedly, rolling up the flank of the already occupied enemy. The remaining peasants rode on in unmolested terror as their pursuers turned to face the assault. As the horse barbarians rallied, the knights began to give back toward the castle.

And from a roof, a huddled half-frozen girl cried out with her mind, "Nils, Nils, come and get me."

6.

This gray dawn was the coldest yet, and the horses' hooves sounded sharply on the frozen ground. There were no clouds. To the east the sky shone yellow along the line of hills as they rode southward down the road. Ilse was draped with a sleeping robe dropped at a door by a horse barbarian and snatched up by Nils as the three warriors had galloped through the village to get her. Now Sten, having circled eastward, caught up with them.

Hannes, he said, had stayed with his surviving peasants, leading them into the forest.

"And what will happen to them?" Ilse asked. "Will the enemy hunt them down?"

Nils smiled. "The first thing the enemy will do is see what horses he can find. It won't be many; mostly peasant plow horses." He turned to Sten. "How many horse barbarians died, do you think?"

Sten answered in Swedish so that Leif and Erik could understand. "I'd guess maybe twenty were killed this afternoon with arrows from the roofs, but that's just a guess. I watched from a hedgerow, but not very close. And tonight Hannes' peasants must have tallied twenty or more killed. Killed or maimed, that is. Their strokes weren't too accurate, and I kept worrying they'd fall off their horses. But even peasants can be effective with an advantage like that.

"The knights must have killed ten or a dozen when they hit, and maybe a few more getting back to the castle. And the archers at the castle might have gotten lucky in the moonlight and knocked off a few more if they followed too close to the walls. How many does that come to?"

"Fifty or sixty," Nils answered. "And we killed four paddock guards and maybe half a dozen in the village when we rode in to get Ilse. And we killed horses until my sword arm got so tired I had to switch hands."

He turned to Ilse. "We'll have to teach you Swedish now. Our people don't know Anglic."

"Perhaps we should teach Leif and Erik Anglic, too." She smiled when she said it, but Nils sensed something behind the words. "I had a precognition weeks ago," she went on. "Men will come out of the sky in a starship, men like the ancients, speaking Anglic, and they will come among your people."

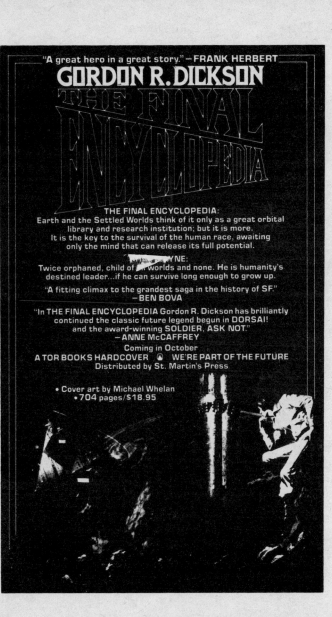

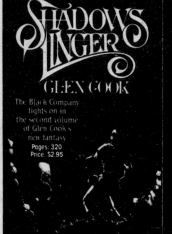